**George Thompson**

# My Life

Outlook

**George Thompson**

# My Life

1. Auflage | ISBN: 978-3-73262-965-7

Erscheinungsort: Frankfurt am Main, Deutschland

Erscheinungsjahr: 2018

Outlook Verlag GmbH, Frankfurt.

# MY LIFE:

**OR**

# THE ADVENTURES OF GEO. THOMPSON. BEING THE AUTO-BIOGRAPHY OF AN AUTHOR. WRITTEN BY HIMSELF.

Why rove in *Fiction's* shadowy land,
  And seek for treasures there,
When *Truth's* domain, so near at hand,
  Is filled with things most rare—
When every day brings something new,
Some great, stupendous change,
Something exciting, wild and *true*,
Most wonderful and strange!

[ORIGINAL.]

**{First published 1854}**

**Yellow Cover of Thompson's My Life. Original size 6 x 9-$^1/_8$". Courtesy, American Antiquarian Society.**

---

# INTRODUCTION

***In which the author defineth his position.***

It having become the fashion of distinguished novelists to write their own lives—or, in other words, to blow their own trumpets,—the author of these pages is induced, at the solicitation of numerous friends, whose bumps of inquisitiveness are strongly developed, to present his auto-biography to the public—in so doing which, he but follows the example of Alexandre Dumas, the brilliant French novelist, and of the world-renowned Dickens, both of whom are understood to be preparing their personal histories for the press.

Now, in comparing myself with the above great worthies, who are so deservedly distinguished in the world of literature, I shall be accused of unpardonable presumption and ridiculous egotism—but I care not what may be said of me, inasmuch as a total independence of the opinions, feelings and prejudices of the world, has always been a prominent characteristic of mine—and that portion of the world and the "rest of mankind" which does not like me, has my full permission to go to the devil as soon as it can make all the necessary arrangements for the journey.

I shall be true and candid, in these pages. I shall not seek to conceal one of my numerous faults which I acknowledge and deplore; and, if I imagine that I possess one solitary merit, I shall not be backward in making that merit known. Those who know me personally, will never accuse me of entertaining one single atom of that despicable quality, self-conceit; those who do not know me, are at liberty to think what they please.—Heaven knows that had I possessed a higher estimation of myself, a more complete reliance upon my own powers, and some of that universal commodity known as "cheek," I should at this present moment have been far better off in fame and fortune. But I have been unobtrusive, unambitious, retiring—and my friends have blamed me for this a thousand times. I have seen writers of no talent at all— petty scribblers, wasters of ink and spoilers of paper, who could not write six consecutive lines of English grammar, and whose short paragraphs for the newspapers invariably had to undergo revision and correction—I have seen such fellows causing themselves to be invited to public banquets and other festivals, and forcing their unwelcome presence into the society of the most distinguished men of the day.

I have spoken of my friends—now a word or two in regard to my enemies. Like most men who have figured before the public, in whatever capacity, I have secured the hatred of many persons, who, jealous of my humble fame, have lost no opportunity of spitting out their malice and opposing my progress. The friendship of such persons is a misfortune—their enmity is a blessing.

I assure them that their hatred will never cause me to lose a fraction of my appetite, or my nightly rest. They may consider themselves very fortunate, if, in the following pages, they do not find themselves immortalized by my notice, although they are certainly unworthy of so great a distinction. I enjoy the friendship of men of letters, and am therefore not to be put down by the opposition of a parcel of senseless blockheads, without brain, or heart, or soul.

I shall doubtless find it necessary to make allusions to local places, persons, incidents, &c. Those will add greatly to the interest of the narrative. Many portraits will be readily recognized, especially those whose originals reside in Boston, where the greater portion of my literary career has been passed.

*The life of an author*, must necessarily be one of peculiar and absorbing interest, for he dwells in a world of his own creation, and his tastes, habits, and feelings are different from those of other people. How little is he understood—how imperfectly is he appreciated, by a cold, unsympathising world! his eccentricities are ridiculed—his excesses are condemned by unthinking persons, who cannot comprehend the fact that a writer, whose mind is weary, naturally longs for physical excitement of some kind of other, and too often seeks for a temporary mental oblivion in the intoxicating bowl. Under any and every circumstance, the author is certainly deserving of some degree of charitable consideration, because he labors hard for the public entertainment, and draws heavily on the treasures of his imagination, in order to supply the continual demands of the reading community. When the author has led a life of stirring adventure, his history becomes one of extraordinary and thrilling interest. I flatter myself that this narrative will be found worthy of the reader's perusal.

And now a few words concerning my personal identity. Many have insanely supposed me to be George Thompson, the celebrated English abolitionist and member of the British Parliament, but such cannot be the case, that individual having returned to his own country. Again—others have taken me for George Thompson, the pugilist; but by far the greater part of the performers in this interesting "Comedy of Errors" have imagined me to be no less a personage than the celebrated "*One-eyed Thompson*," and they long continued in this belief, even after that talented but most unfortunate man had committed suicide in New York, and in spite of the fact that his name was William H., and not George. Two circumstances, however, seemed to justify the belief before the man's death:—he, like myself, had the great misfortune to be deprived of an eye. How the misfortune happened to *me*, I shall relate in the proper place. I have written many works of fiction, but I have passed through adventures quite as extraordinary as any which I have drawn from the imagination.

In order to establish my claim to the title of "author," I will enumerate a few of the works which I have written:—

Gay Girls of New York, Dissipation, The Housekeeper, Venus in Boston, Jack Harold, Criminal, Outlaw, Road to Ruin, Brazen Star, Kate Castleton, Redcliff, The Libertine, City Crimes, The Gay Deceiver, Twin Brothers, Demon of Gold, Dashington, Lady's Garter, Harry Glindon, Catharine and Clara.

In addition to these works—which have all met with a rapid sale and most extensive circulation—I have written a sufficient quantity of tales, sketches, poetry, essays and other literary stock of every description, to constitute halfa dozen cart loads. My adventures, however, and not my productions must employ my pen; and begging the reader's pardon for this rather lengthy, but very necessary, introduction, I begin my task.

# CHAPTER I

***In which I begin to Acquire a Knowledge of the World.***

I have always thought, and still think, that it matters very little where or when a man is born—it is sufficient for him to know that he is *here*, and that he had better adapt himself, as far as possible, to the circumstances by which he is surrounded, provided that he wishes to toddle through the world with comfort and credit to himself and to the approbation of others. But still, in order to please all classes of readers, I will state that some thirty years ago a young stranger struggled into existence in the city of New York; and I will just merely hint that the twenty-eighth day of August, in the year of our Lord one thousand eight hundred and twenty-three, should be inserted in the next (comic) almanac as having been the birth-day of a great man—for when an individual attains a bodily weight of two hundred pounds and over, may he not be styled *great*?

My parents were certainly respectable people, but they both inconsiderately died at a very early period of my life, leaving me a few hundred dollars and a thickheaded uncle, to whom was attached an objectionable aunt, the proprietress of a long nose and a shrewish temper. The nose was adapted to the consumption of snuff, and the temper was effective in the destruction of my happiness and peace of mind. The worthy couple, with a prophetic eye, saw that I was destined to become, in future years, somewhat of a *gourmand*, unless care should be taken to prevent such a melancholy fate; therefore, actuated by the best motives, and in order to teach me the luxury of abstinence, they began by slow but sure degrees to starve me. Good people, how I reverence their memory!

One night I committed burglary upon a closet, and feloniously carried off a chunk of bread and meat, which I devoured in the cellar.

"Oh, my prophetic soul—*my uncle*!" That excellent man caught me in the act of eating the provender, and—my bones ache at this very moment as I think of the licking I got! I forgot to mention that I had a rather insignificant brother, four years older than myself, who became my uncle's apprentice, and who joined that gentleman in his persecutions against me. My kind relatives were rather blissful people in the way of ignorance, and they hated me because they imagined that I regarded myself as their superior—a belief that was founded on the fact that I shunned their society and passed the greater portion of my time in reading and writing.

I lived at that time in Thomas street, very near the famous brothel of Rosina Townsend, in whose house that dreadful murder was committed which the New York public will still remember with a thrill of horror. I allude to the murder of the celebrated courtezan Ellen Jewett. Her lover, Richard P. Robinson, was tried and acquitted of the murder, through the eloquence of his talented counsel, Ogden Hoffman, Esq. The facts of the case are briefly these: —Robinson was a clerk in a wholesale store, and was the paramour of Ellen, who was strongly attached to him. Often have I seen them walking together, both dressed in the height of fashion, the beautiful Ellen leaning upon the arm of the dashing Dick, while their elegant appearance attracted universal attention and admiration. But all this soon came to a bloody termination. Dick was engaged to be married to a young lady of the highest respectability, the heiress of wealth and the possessor of surpassing loveliness. He informed Ellen that his connection with her must cease in consequence of his matrimonial arrangements, whereupon Ellen threatened to expose him to his "intended" if he abandoned her. Embarrassed by the critical nature of his situation, Dick, then, in an evil hour, resolved to kill the courtezan who threatened to destroy his anticipated happiness. One Saturday night he visited her as usual; and after a splendid supper, they returned to her chamber. Upon that occasion, as was afterwards proved on the trial, Dick wore an ample cloak, and several persons noticed that he seemed to have something concealed beneath it. His manner towards Ellen and also his words, were that night unusually caressing and affectionate. What passed in that chamber, and who perpetrated that murder the Almighty knows—*and, perhaps, Dick Robinson, if he is still alive, also knows*![A] The next morning (Sunday,) at a very early hour, smoke was seen to proceed from Ellen's chamber, and the curtains of her bed were found to have been set on fire. The flames were with difficulty extinguished, and there in the half consumed bed, was found the mangled corpse of Ellen Jewett, having on the side of her head an awful wound, which had evidently been inflicted by a hatchet. Dick Robinson was nowhere to be found, but in the garden, near a fence, were discovered his cloak and a bloody hatchet. With many others, I entered the room in which lay the body of Ellen, and never shall I forget the horrid spectacle that met my gaze! There, upon that couch of sin, which had been scathed by fire, lay blackened the half-burned remains of a once-beautiful woman, whose head exhibited the dreadful wound which had caused her death. It had plainly been the murderer's intention to burn down the house in order to destroy the ghastly evidence of his crime; but fate ordained that the fire should be discovered and extinguished before the *fatal wound* became obliterated. Robinson, as I said before, was tried and pronounced guiltless of the crime, through the ingenuity of his counsel, who termed him an "*innocent boy*." The public, however, firmly believed in his guilt; and the question arises—"If

Dick Robinson did not kill Ellen Jewett, *who did*?" I do not believe that ever before was presented so shameful an instance of perverted justice, or so striking an illustration of the "glorious uncertainty of the law." It is rather singular that Furlong, a grocer, who swore to an *alibi* in favor of Robinson, and who was the chief instrument employed to effect the acquittal of that young man, some time afterwards committed suicide by drowning, having first declared that his conscience reproached him for the part which he played at the trial!

The Sabbath upon which this murder was brought to light was a dark, stormy day, and I have reason to remember it well, for, in the afternoon, that good old pilgrim—my uncle, of course,—discovered that I had played truant from Sunday School in the morning, and for that atrocious crime, he, in his holy zeal for my spiritual and temporal welfare, resolved to bestow upon me a wholesome and severe flogging, being aided and abetted in the formation of that laudable resolution by my religious aunt and my sanctimonious brother, the latter of whom had turned *informer* against me. Sweet relatives? how I love to think of them—and never do I fail to remember them in my prayers. Well, I was lugged up into the garret, which was intended to be the scene of my punishment. If I recollect rightly, I was then about twelve years of age, and rather a stout youth considering my years. I determined to rebel against the authority of my beloved kindred, assert my independence, and defend myself to the best of my ability. "I have suffered enough;" said I to myself, "and now I'm *going in*."

"Sabbath-breaker, strip off your jacket," mildly remarked by dear uncle as he savagely flourished a cowhide of most formidable aspect and alarming suppleness.

My reply was brief, but expressive:

"I'll see you d——d first," said I.

My uncle turned pale, my aunt screamed, and my brother rolled up the white of his eyes and groaned.

"What, what did you say?" demanded my uncle, who could not believe the evidence of his own senses, for up to that moment I had always tamely submitted to the good man's amiable treatment of me, and he found it impossible to imagine that I was capable of resisting him. Well, if there ever *was* an angel on earth, that uncle of mine was that particular angel. Saints in general are provided with pinched noses, green eyes, and voices like unto the wailings of a small pig, which is suffering the agonies of death beneath a cart-wheel. And, if there ever was a cherub, my brother *was* certainly that individual cherub, although, in truth, my pious recollections do not furnish me with the statement that cherubs are remarkable for swelled heads and bandy legs.

"I say," was my reply to my uncle's astonished inquiry, "that I ain't going to stand any more abuse and beatings. I've stood bad treatment long enough from the whole pack of you. I'm almost starved, and I'm kicked about like a dog. Let any of you three tyrants touch me, and I'll show you what is to get desperate. I disown you all as relatives, and hereafter I'm going to live where I please, and do as I please."

Furious with rage, my sweet-tempered uncle raised the cowhide and with it struck me across the face. I immediately pitched into that portion of his person where he was accustomed to stow away his Sabbath beans, and the excellent man fell head over heels down the garret stairs, landing securely at the bottom and failing to pick himself up, for the simple reason that he had broken his leg. What a pity it would have been, and what a loss society would have sustained, if, instead of his leg, the holy man had broken his *neck*!

My dear brother, accompanied by my affectionate aunt, now choked me, but I was not to be conquered just then, for "thrice is he armed who hath his quarrel just." The lady I landed in a tub of impure water that happened to be standing near; and she presented quite an interesting appearance, kicking up her heels and squalling like a cat in difficulties. My other assailant I hurled into a heap of ashes, and the way he blubbered was a caution to a Nantucket whaleman. Rushing down the stairs, I passed over the prostrate form of my crippled uncle, who requested me to come back, so that he might kick me with his serviceable foot; but, brute that I was, I disregarded him—requested him to go to a place which shall be nameless—and then left the house as expeditiously as possible, fully determined never to return, whatever might be the consequences.

"I am now old enough, and big enough," I mentally reflected, "to take care of myself; and to-morrow I'll look for work, and try to get a chance to learn a trade. Where shall I sleep to-night? It's easy enough to ask that question, but deuced hard to answer it. I wish to-day wasn't Sunday!"

Rather an impious wish, but quite natural under the circumstances. I felt in my pockets, to see if I was the proprietor of any loose change; my search was magnificently successful, for I discovered that I had a sixpence!

Yes, reader, a new silver sixpence, that glittered in my hand like a bright star of hope, urging me on to enterprise—to exertions. So fearful was I of losing the precious coin, that I continued to grasp it tightly in my hand. I never had been allowed any pocket money, even on the Fourth of July; and this large sum had come into my possession through the munificence of a neighbor, as a reward for performing an errand.

Not knowing where else to go, I went down on the Battery, and sheltered myself under a tree from the rain, which fell in torrents. Rather an interesting situation for a youth of twelve—homeless, friendless, almost penniless! I was wet through to the skin, and as night came on, I became desperately hungry, for I had eaten no dinner that day, and even my breakfast had been of the *phantom* order—something like the pasteboard meals which are displayed upon the stage of the theatre. However, I did not despair, for I was young and active, full of the hope so natural to a youth ere rough contact with the world has crushed his spirit. I was well aware of the fact that I was no fool, although I had often been called one by my hostile and unappreciating relatives, whose opinions I had ever held in most supreme contempt. As I stood under that tree to shelter myself from the rain, I felt quite happy, for a feeling of independence had arisen within me. I was now my own master, and the consciousness that I must solely rely upon myself, was to me a source of gratification and pride. I had not the slightest doubt of being able to dig my way through the world in some way or other.

Night came on at last, black as the brow of a Congo nigger, and starless as a company of travelling actors. I could not remain under the tree all night, that was certain; and so I left it, although I could scarcely see my hand before me. That hand, by the way, still tenaciously grasped the invaluable sixpence. Groping my way out of the Battery, and guided by a light, I entered the bar-room of a respectable hotel, where a large number of well-dressed gentlemen were assembled, who were seeking shelter from the storm, and at the same time indulging their convivial propensities. Much noise and confusion prevailed; and two gentlemen, who, as I afterwards learned, were officers belonging to a Spanish vessel then in port, fell into a dispute and got into a fight, during which one of them stabbed the other with a dirk-knife, inflicting a mortal wound.

Officers were sent for, the murderer and his victim were removed, and comparative quiet prevailed. I was seated in an obscure corner of the bar-room, wondering how I should get through the night, when I was unceremoniously accosted by a lad of about my own age. He was a rakish looking youth, quite handsome withal, dressed in the height of fashion, and was smoking a cigar with great vigor and apparent relish. It will be seen hereafter that I have reason to remember this individual to the very last day of my life. Would to heaven that I had never met him!

This youth slapped me familiarly on the shoulder, and said—

"Hallo, bub! why, you're wet as a drowned rat! Come and take a brandy cocktail—it will warm you up!"

I had never drank a drop of liquor in my life, and I hadn't the faintest idea of what a brandy cocktail was, and so I told my new friend, who laughed immoderately as he exclaimed—

"How jolly green you are, to be sure; why, you're a regular *greenhorn*, and I'm going to call you by that name hereafter. Have you got any tin?"

I knew that he meant money, and so I told him that I had but a sixpence in the world.

"Bah!" cried my friend, as he drew his cigar from his mouth and salivated in the most fashionable manner, "who are you, what are you and what are you doing here? Come, tell me all about yourself, and it may perhaps be in my power to do you a service."

His frank, off-hand manner won my confidence. I told him my whole story, without any reserve; and he laughed uproariously when I told him how I had pitched my tyrannical uncle down stairs.

"It served the old chap right," said he approvingly—"you are a fellow of some spirit, and I like you. Come take a drink, and we can afterwards talk over what is best to be done."

I objected to drink, because I had formed a strong prejudice against ardent spirits, having often been a witness of its deplorable effects in depriving men —and women, too—of their reason, and reducing them to the condition of brute beasts. So, in declining my friend's invitation, I told him my reasons for so doing, whereupon he laughed louder than ever, as he remarked—

"Why, *Greenhorn*, you'd make an excellent temperance lecturer. But perhaps you think I haven't got any money to pay the rum. Look here—what do you think of *that*?"

He displayed a large roll of bank bills, and flourished them triumphantly. I had never before seen so much money, except in the broker's windows; and my friend was immediately established in my mind as a *millionaire*, whose wealth was inexhaustible. I suddenly conceived for him the most profound respect, and would not have offended him for the world. How could I persist in refusing to drink with a young gentleman of such wealth, and (as a necessary consequence) such distinction? Besides, I suddenly felt quite a curiosity to drink some liquor, just to see how it tasted. After all, it was only very low people who got drunk and wallowed in the mire. *Gentlemen* (I thought) never get drunk, and they always seem so happy and joyous after they have been drinking! How they shake hands, and swear eternal friendship, and seem generously willing to lend or give away all they have in the world! So thought I, as my mind was made up to accept the invitation of my friend. It is singular that I had forgotten all about the murder which had just taken place in that bar-room, and which had been directly produced by intemperance.

"The fact is, my dear *Greenhorn*," said my friend, impressively, as he flourished his hand after the manner of some aged, experienced and eloquent orator, "the fact is, the *use* of liquor, and its *abuse*, are two very different things. A man (here he drew himself up) can drink like a gentleman, or he can swill like a loafer, or a beast. Now *I* prefer the gentlemanly portion of the argument, and therefore we'll go up and take a gentlemanly drink. I shall be happy, young man, to initiate you into the divine joys and mysteries of Bacchus—ahem!"

I looked at my friend with increased wonder, for he displayed an assurance, a self-possession, an elegant *nonchalance*, that were far beyond his years, for he was only about twelve years old—my own age exactly. And then what language he used—so refined, glowing, and indicative of a knowledge of the world! I longed to be like him—to equal him in his many perfections—to sport as much money as he did, and to wear as good "*harness*." I forgot to mention that he carried a splendid gold watch, and that several glittering rings adorned his fingers. "Who can he be?" was the question which I asked myself; and of course, I could not find an answer.

"Felix," said my friend, addressing the bar-keeper in a style of patronizing condescension, as we approached the bar, "Felix, my good fellow, just mix us a couple of brandy cocktails, will you, and make them *strong*, d'ye hear, for the night is wet, and I and my verdant friend here, are about to travel in search of amusement, even as the Caliph and his Vizier used to perambulate the streets of Baghdad. Come, hurry up!"

The bar-keeper grinned, mixed the liquor, and handed us the tumblers. My friend knocked his glass against mine, and remarked "here's luck," a ceremony and an observation which both somewhat surprised me at the time, although I have long since become thoroughly acquainted with what was then a mystery. Many of my readers—indeed, I may say the greater portion of them—will require no explanation of this matter; and as for those who are in ignorance of it, I will simply say, long may they keep so!

My friend tossed off his cocktail with the air of one who is used to it, and rather liked it than otherwise; but I was not quite so successful, for being wholly unacquainted with the science of drinking, the strength of the liquor nearly choked me, to the intense amusement of my more experienced friend, who advised me to try again. I *did* try again, and more successfully, the liquor went the way of all rum, and soon produced the usual effects. Of course its influence on me was exceedingly powerful, I being entirely unaccustomed to its use. A very agreeable feeling of exhilaration stole over me—I thought I was worth just one hundred thousand dollars—I embraced my friend and swore he was a "trump"—I then noticed, with mild surprise, that he had been multiplied into two individuals—there were two barkeepers now, although just before I drank, there was but one—an additional chandelier had just stepped in to visit the solitary one which had lighted the room—to speak plainly, I saw double; and to sum the whole matter up in a few words, I was, for the first time in my life, most decidedly and incontestably *drunk*.

As nearly as I can remember, my friend linked his arm within mine, and we passed out into the street—he partially supporting me, and keeping me from falling. Two precious youths, of twelve years of age, we certainly were—one staggering and trying to fall down, and the other laughing, and holding him up!

The rain had ceased falling, and the stars were shining as if nothing had happened. The cool air sobered me, and my friend congratulated me on my recovery from a state of inebriety.

"After a little practice at the bar," said he—"it will take a good many *tods* to *floor* you. Let me give you a few hints as regards drinking. Never mix your liquor—always stick to one kind. After every glass, eat a cracker—or, what is better, a pickle. Plain drinks are always the best—far preferable to fancy drinks, which contain sugar, and lemons, and mint, and other trash; although a mixed drink may be taken on a stormy night, such as this has been. Drink ale, or beer, sparingly, and only after dinner—for, taken in large quantities, it is apt to bloat a person, and it plays the very devil with his internal arrangements. Besides, it is filthy stuff, at best, being made of the most repulsive materials and in the dirtiest manner. Always drink *good liquor*, which will not hurt you, while the vile stuff which is sold in the different bar- rooms will soon send you to your grave. If you pass a day or two in drinking freely, do not miss eating a single meal, and if you do not feel inclined to eat, *force* yourself to do it; for, if you neglect your food, that terrible fiend, *Delirium Tremens*, will have you in his savage grasp before you know it. Every morning after a *spree*, take a good stiff horn of brandy, and soon afterwards a glass of plain soda, which will cool you off. Never drink gin—it is vulgar stuff, not fit to be used by gentlemen.—When you desire to reform from drinking, never break off abruptly, which is dangerous; but *taper off* gradually—three glasses to-day, two to-morrow, and one the next day. Never drink with low people, under any circumstances, for it brings you down to their level. When you go to a drinking party, or to a fashionable dinner, sit with your back toward the sun—confine yourself to one kind of liquor—take an occasional sip of vinegar—and the very devil himself cannot drink you under the table! Now do you understand me, my dear *greenhorn*?"

Such language and advice, emanating from a boy of twelve, astonished me, and hurried me to the conclusion that he must be a very "*fast*" youth indeed. I took a more particular survey of my new friend. He was not remarkable handsome, but his face was flushing not with health, but with drinking. A rosy tint suffused his full cheeks, and a delicate vermillion colored the top of his well-formed nose. His form was somewhat slighter than mine, but he looked vigorous and active. His closely buttoned jacket developed a full breast, and a pair of muscular arms. His small feet were encased in patent-leather boots. Upon his head was a jaunty cloth cap, from beneath which flowed a quantity of fine, curly hair. I really envied him his good looks, as also his mental endowments. He saw that I admired him; and he liked me for it.

Such was *Jack Slack*, I may as well give his name at once, for I hate the trickery of authors who keep the curiosity of their readers painfully excited to the end of their narratives for the purpose of producing an *effect*. My professional habits as a writer prompt me to do the same; but I must not forget that I am writing my own history, and not an effusion of my imagination, which seems to be a prolific mother, for it hath produced many children, and (if I live) may produce many more.

While I now write, the Sabbath bells are ringing in sweet harmony, and through my open window comes the cool but mild breath of an autumnal morning. Yes, it is Sunday, and all the holy associations of the sacred day crowd upon me. I can almost see the village church, and the throng of worshippers within it, listening to the fervent remarks and exhortations of their pastor. Then I can fancy the gorgeous cathedral, with its stained windows, its elaborate carvings, its pealing organs, and its fashionable assembly of superficial worshippers. While others are praying, pleasuring and sleeping, I am rushing my iron pen over the spotless paper, and wishing that my penmanship could keep pace with my thought.—This is a digression; but the reader will pardon it. There is *one* dear creature, I know, who, when her eyes scan these pages, will understand me. But she, alas! is far away.

Where was I? Oh, speaking of Jack Slack. How well do I remember the night upon which first I met him! I can see him now, with his mischievous smiles, his eyes full of deviltry—his scornful lips—I can almost hear his mocking laugh. Yes, although eighteen years have passed since then, the remembrance of that night is fresh within me, as if its occurrence were but things of yesterday.

May perdition seize the circumstances which led me to encounter him! He was the foundation of my misfortunes in life. But for him, I might have led a happy, tranquil life; unknown, it is true, but still happy. But, poor fellow! he is dead now. He died by my hand, and I do not regret the act, nor would I recall it, had I the power. But of this the reader shall know hereafter.

That was my first night of dissipation—that was the occasion of my initiation into the mysteries of debauchery. I had previously led a necessarily regular and abstemious life—to bed at eight, up at six, at school by nine, and so on. (By the way, I never learned any thing at school—the master pronounced me the most stupid rascal in the concern; and flogged me accordingly—good old man! All I ever learned was acquired in a *printing office.*) Well, here was I at the age of twelve, fairly launched upon the sea of city life, without a guide, protector, or friend. What wonder is it that I became a reckless, dissipated individual, careless of myself, my interests, my fame and fortune?

Jack Slack and I, arm-in-arm, entered Broadway, and proceeded at a leisurely pace up that noble avenue. Many a courtezan did we meet, and many a watchman did we salute with the compliments of the season. (There were no *Brazen Stars*,[B] nor *M.P. 's*, then.) One lady of the pave, whom my companion addressed in terms of complimentary gallantry, said—"Little boy, go home to your mother and tell her she wants you!"

I am now about to make a humiliating confession, but I must not shrink from it, inasmuch as I sat down with the determination of writing "the truth, the whole truth, and nothing but the truth." I allowed Jack to persuade me to accompany him on a visit to a celebrated establishment in Leonard street—a house occupied by accommodating ladies of great personal attractions, who were not especially virtuous. That was of course my first visit to a house of ill-fame; and without exactly comprehending the nature of the place and its arrangements, I was deeply impressed with the strangeness and novelty of everything that surrounded me. The costly and elegant furniture—the brilliant chandeliers—the magnificent but rather *loose* French prints and paintings—the universal luxury that prevailed—the voluptuous ladies, with their bare shoulders, painted cheeks, and free-and-easy manners—the buxom, bustling landlady, who was dressed with almost regal splendor and wore a profusion of jewelry—the crowd of half-drunken gentlemen who were drinking wine and laughing uproariously—all these things astonished and bewildered me. My friend Jack appeared to be well known to the inmates of the house, with whom he seemed to be an immense favorite. Having—much to my dissatisfaction and disgust—introduced me to a lady, he took possession of another one, and called for a couple of bottles of wine. Jack and his lady were evidently upon the most intimate and affectionate terms, while my female companion seemed inclined to be very loving, but I did not appreciate her advances, being altogether unaccustomed to such things. The champagne was brought, and I was persuaded to drink freely of it. The consequence was that I soon became helplessly intoxicated. I can indistinctly remember the dancing lights, the popping of champagne corks—the noise, the confusion, the thrumming of a piano, and the boisterous laughter—and then I fell into a condition of complete insensibility.

When I awoke, I was astonished at my situation and naturally enough, for I was in a strange apartment and snugly stowed away in a strange but decidedly luxuriant bed. The room was handsomely furnished, but to my additional surprise, many female garments were scattered about, indicating that the regular inhabitant of the place was a lady. This mystery was soon solved, forI was not the only inmate of the couch. My companion was the lady to whom I had been introduced by Jack Slack. Pitying my helpless condition—and, doubtless, prompted by the mischievous Jack—she had carried me to bed, and had also retired herself, being actuated by a benevolent anxiety for my safety. What a delicate situation for a modest youth to be placed in! Having, to my no small satisfaction, ascertained that the lady was fast asleep, I arose so carefully and noiselessly as not to awaken her. In truth, I was disgusted with the whole concern, and determined to leave it as speedily as possible. A light was fortunately burning in the room, which enabled me to move about with safety. A gold watch which lay upon the table informed me that it was nearly midnight.—Leaving the chamber and its sleeping inmate, I crept down stairs, and, on passing the door of the principal sitting-room, the voice of Jack Slack, who was singing a comic song amid the most enthusiastic applause, convinced me that my interesting friend was still rendering himself a source of amusement and an object of admiration. Without stopping to compliment him upon the excellence of his performance, I approached the front door, turned the key which was in the lock, unfastened the chain, and passed out into the street, just as the clock of a neighboring steeple was proclaiming the hour of twelve.

My head ached terribly after the champagne which I had so profusely drank, and besides, I felt heavy and sleepy to an extraordinary degree. Unable to resist the overpowering influence of my feelings, I sat down upon the steps of a house and was fast asleep in less than a minute. Then I dreamed of being seized in the powerful grasp of some gigantic demon, and hurried away to the bottomless pit. I certainly felt conscious of being moved about, but my oblivious condition would not admit of arriving at any definite understanding of what was happening to me. When I finally awoke, I found myself in an apartment that was far different in its aspect from the luxurious chamber I had just quitted. The floor, walls and ceiling of the apartment were of stone; there were no windows, but a narrow aperture, high up in the wall, admitted the feeble glimmer of daylight. There was an iron door, and a water-pipe, and platform on which I lay, and on which reposed several gentlemen of seedy raiment and unwholesome appearance. The place and the company, as dimly revealed by the uncertain morning light, inspired me with emotions of horror; and in my inexperience and ignorance, I said to myself—

"I must leave this place at once. How I came here is a mystery, but it is certain that I cannot remain."

I arose from my hard couch, and approached the iron door with the confident expectation of being able to pass out without any difficulty, for I imagined that I had fallen into one of those cheap and wretched lodging houses with which the city abounds. (By the way, I may hereafter have something to say with reference to these cheap lodging-houses. Some rich development may be made, which will rather astonish the unsophisticated reader.)

To my surprise, I found that the door could not be opened; and then one of my fellow-lodgers, who had been observing my movements, exclaimed:

"Are you going to leave us, my lad? Then leave us your card, or a lock of your hair to remember you by."

"Will you be kind enough to tell me what place this is?" said I.

The man laughed loudly, as he replied—

"Why, don't you know? What an innocent youth you are, to be sure! How the devil could you come here, without knowing anything about it? But I suppose that you were drunk, which is a great pity for a boy like you. Well, not to keep you in suspense, I must inform you that you are in the *watch-house of the Tombs*!"

This information appalled me. To be in confinement—to be a prisoner—to be associated with a company of outcasts, thieves and perhaps murderers—was to me the height of horror. I looked particularly at the man with whom I had been conversing. He was a savage-looking individual, with a beard like that of a pirate, and an eye that spoke of blood and outrage. He was roughly dressed, in a garb that announced him to be a mariner.

In the course of a conversation that we fell into, he informed me that he had committed a murder on the preceding evening, and that he expected to be hung.

"We quarrelled at cards," said he, "and he gave me the lie—whereupon I drew my death-knife and stabbed him to the heart. He died instantly; the police rushed in, and here I am. My neck will be stretched, but I don't care. What matters it how a man dies? When my time comes, I shall go forth as readily and as cheerfully as if I were going to take a drink."

(I will here remark that I afterwards saw this man hung in the yard of the *Tombs*. His history is in my possession, and I shall hereafter write it.)[C]

At nine o'clock I was taken before the magistrate, who, after severely reprimanding me for my misconduct, discharged me from custody, with the remark that if I were brought there again he would be obliged to commit me to the Tombs for the term of five days. Delighted at having obtained my liberty, I posted out of the court room and found myself in Centre street. My debauch of the preceding night had not spoiled my appetite, by any means; and, as I still had in my possession the sixpence alluded to before, I resolved to produce some breakfast forthwith. Aware that my limited finances would not admit of my obtaining a very sumptuous repast, and fully appreciating the necessity of economy, I entered the shop of a baker and purchased three rolls at the rate of one cent per copy. Thus provided, I repaired to a neighboring street pump, and made a light but wholesome breakfast.

It was thus, reader, that your humble servant began to acquire a knowledge of the world.

## FOOTNOTES:

[A] The last that was heard of Robinson, he was in Texas, and it was reported that he was married and wealthy, his right arm he had lost in some battle, the name of which I do not remember.

[B] I have just written a story under this title, full of fact and fun, and containing more truth than poetry. The reader can have it by applying to the publisher of this work. It is well worthy of perusal.

[C] This work is now in active course of preparation. To the lovers of exciting tales, this story will be one of particular attraction. It will be issued by the publisher of this narrative.

---

# CHAPTER II

***In which I become a Printer, and am introduced into certain mysteries of connubial life.***

Having breakfasted to my entire satisfaction and also to my great bodily refreshment, I entered the Park, seated myself upon the steps of the City Hall, and thought "what is best to be done?"—It was Monday morning, and the weather was excellently fine. It was an excellent time to search for employment. A sign on an old building in Chatham street attracted my notice; upon it were inscribed the words, "Book and Job Printing."

"Good!" was my muttered exclamation, as I left the Park and crossed over towards the old building in question—"I'll be a printer! Franklin was one, and he, like myself, was fond of rolls, because he entered Philadelphia with one under each arm. Yes, I'll be a printer."

Entering the printing office, I found it to be a very small concern, containing but one press and a rather limited assortment of type. The proprietor of the office, whom I shall call Mr. Romaine, was a rather intellectual looking man, of middle age. Being very industrious, he did the principal portion of his work himself, occasionally, however, hiring a journeyman when work was unusually abundant. As I entered he looked up from his case and inquired, with an air of benevolence—

"Well, my lad, what can I do for *you* this morning?"

"If you please, sir, I want to learn to be a printer," replied I, boldly.

"Ah, indeed! Well, I was just thinking of taking an apprentice. But give an account of yourself—how old are you, and who are you?"

I frankly communicated to Mr. Romaine all that he desired to know concerning me, and he expressed himself as being perfectly satisfied. He immediately set me to "learning the boxes" of a case of type; and in half an hour I had accomplished the task, which was not very difficult, it being merely an effort of memory.

It having been arranged that I should take up my abode in the house of Mr. Romaine, I accompanied that gentleman home to dinner. He lived in William street and his wife kept a fashionable boarding-house for merchants, professional men, &c. Several of these gentlemen were married men and had their wives with them. Mrs. Romaine, the wife of my employer, was one of the finest-looking women I ever saw—tall, voluptuous, and truly beautiful.

She was about twenty-five years of age, and her manners were peculiarly fascinating and agreeable. She was always dressed in a style of great elegance, and was admirably adapted to the station which she filled as landlady of an establishment like that. I will remark that although she had been the wife of Mr. Romaine for a number of years, she had not been blessed with offspring, which was doubtless to her a source of great disappointment, to say nothing of the *chagrin* which a married woman naturally feels when she fails in due time to add to the population of her country.

Accustomed as I had been to the economical scantiness of my uncle's table, I was both surprised and delighted with the luxurious abundance that greeted me on sitting down to dinner at Mrs. Romaine's. I was equally well pleased with the sprightliness, intelligence and good-humor of the conversation in which the ladies and gentlemen engaged, and also with their refined and courteous bearing towards each other. I congratulated myself on having succeeded in getting not only into business, but also into good society.

"If my dearly-beloved relatives," thought I, "could see me now, they might not be well pleased at my situation and prospects. Let them go to Beelzebub! I will get on in the world, in spite of them!"

In a few days I began to be very useful about the printing office, for I had learned to set type and to *roll* behind the press; I also performed all the multifarious duties of *devil*, and was so fortunate as to secure the good will of my employer, who generously purchased for me a fine new suit of clothes, and seemed anxious to make me as comfortable as possible. His wife, also, treated me very kindly; but there was something mysterious about this lady, which for a time, puzzled me extremely. One discovery which I made rather astonished me, young as I was, and caused me to do a "devil of a thinking." Mr. Romaine and his wife occupied separate sleeping apartments, and there seemed to be an aversion between them, although they treated each other with the most formal and scrupulous politeness. But my readers will agree with me that mere *politeness* is not the only sentiment which should exist between a husband and his wife. There was evidently something "rotten in Denmark" between Mr. and Mrs. Romaine, and I determined, if possible, to penetrate the mystery.

Mr. Romaine, who was professedly a pious man, was particularly in favor of "remembering the Sabbath day to keep it holy," and he therefore directed me to be very punctual in attendance at church and Sunday school, and I obeyed his praiseworthy request until visions of literary greatness and renown began to dawn upon me, whereupon, prompted by gingerbread and ambition, and being moreover aided and abetted by another printer's devil of tender years and literary aspirations, I, one Sunday morning, entered the printing office, (of which I kept the key,) and assisted by my companion, set up and worked off one hundred copies of a diminutive periodical just six inches square, containing a *very* brief abstract of the news of the day, a *very* indifferent political leader, and a few *rather* partial theatrical criticisms. This extensive newspaper we issued on three successive Sundays, circulating it among our juvenile friends at the moderate rate of one cent a copy. On the fourth Sunday we were caught in the act of printing our journal by Mr. Romaine himself, who, although he with difficulty refrained from laughing at the fun of the thing, gave us a long lecture on the crime of Sabbath-breaking, and then made us distribute the type, forgetting that we were breaking the Sabbath as much by taking our form to pieces as by putting it together.

Mr. Romaine was also strongly opposed to theatres, but, nevertheless, I visited the "little Frankin" four or five times every week, to see John and Bill Sefton in the "Golden Farmer," and other thrilling melo-dramas, a convenient ally, a garden and a shed enabled me to enter my chamber at any hour during the night, without my employer's becoming aware of my absence from home.

One night after having been to my favorite place of amusement, I returned home about midnight. On entering the garden, I discovered to my surprise a light streaming from the kitchen windows—a very unusual occurrence. I crept softly up to one of the windows, and looking into the kitchen, a scene met my gaze that filled me with astonishment.

Mrs. Romaine, arrayed in her night-dress only, was seated at a table, and at her side was a young gentleman named Anderson, who boarded in the house, and who was a prosperous merchant. His arm was around the lady's waist, and her head rested affectionately upon his shoulder. She looked uncommonly beautiful and voluptuous that night, I thought, young as I was, I wonderednot at the look of passionate admiration with which Anderson regarded his fair companion, upon whose sensual countenance there rested an expression of gratified love. Upon the table were the remains of a supper of which they had evidently partaken; there were also a bottle of wine and two glasses, partially filled. Mrs. Romaine sipped her wine occasionally, as well as her paramour; and the guilty pair seemed to be enjoying themselves highly. It was plain that the lady was resolved to lose nothing by her estrangement from her husband; it was equally plain that between her and Mr. Romaine there existed not the smallest particle of love. I now ceased to wonder why the wedded pair occupied separate apartments; and I came to the conclusion that disappointment in the matter of children was the cause of their mutual aversion. If I were writing a romance instead of a narrative of facts, I would here introduce an imaginary tender conversation between the pair. But as no such conversation took place I have none to describe.

"Well," said I to myself—"this is a pretty state of affairs, truly. I guess that if Mr. Romaine suspected any thing of this kind, there would be the very devil to pay, and no mistake. But it's no business of mine; and so I'll climb into my window and go to bed."

My employer was a very good sort of a man, and I sincerely pitied him on account of his unhappy connubial situation. I turned away from the kitchen window, and began to mount the shed in order to reach my chamber. I had nearly gained the roof of the shed, when a board gave way and I was precipitated to the ground, a distance of about ten feet. Fortunately I sustained no injury; but the noise aroused and alarmed the loving couple in the kitchen. Mrs. Romaine, in her terror and dread of discovery, gave utterance to a slight scream; while Mr. Anderson rushed forth and seized me in a rather powerful grasp. I struggled, and kicked, and strove to extricate myself, but it was all of no use. With many a muttered imprecation Anderson dragged me into the kitchen, and swore that if I did not remain quiet he would stab me to the heart with a dirk-knife that he produced from his pocket.

"You young rascal," said he "who employed you to play the part of a spy? Did Mr. Romaine direct you to watch us? Is he lurking outside, in the garden? If so, let him beware, for I am a desperate man, one not to be trifled with!"

I explained everything to the entire satisfaction of both the gentleman and lady, whose countenances brightened when they found that matters were far from being as bad as they expected.

"Now, my boy," said Anderson, "just do keep perfectly dark about this business, and I'll make your fortune. You shall never want a dollar while I live. As an earnest of what I may hereafter do for you, accept this trifle, which will enable you to gratify your theatre-going propensities to your heart's content."

The "trifle" was a ten dollar gold piece. I had never before possessed so much money; and no millionaire ever felt richer than I did at that moment. Delightful visions of dramatic treats arose before me, and I was happy.

Mr. Anderson made me drink a couple of glasses of wine, which tasted very good, and caused me to feel quite elevated. Then he told me that I had better go to bed, and I fully agreed with him. So, bidding the enamoured couple a patronizing good night and facetiously wishing them a pleasant time together —the wine had made me bold and saucy—I left the kitchen and began to ascend the stairs towards my own room with all the silence and caution of which I was capable.

I was destined that night to make another astonishing discovery. Being quite tipsy, I was deprived of my usual judgement, and suffered myself to stumble against a table that stood upon one of the landings opposite the chamber door of a young and particularly pretty widow named Mrs. Raymond, who boarded in the house. She possessed a snug independent fortune, and led a life of elegant leisure. Although demure in her looks and reverend in her deportment, there was a whole troop of dancing devils in her eyes that proclaimed the fact that her nature was not exactly as cold as ice.

My collision with the table caused me to recoil, and I fell violently against Mrs. Raymond's door, which burst open, and down I landed in the very centre of the apartment.

I heard a scream, and then a curse. The scream was the performance of the fair widow; the curse was the production of Mr. Romaine, my pious, Sabbath-venerating and theatre-opposing employer, who, springing up from the sofa upon which he had been seated by the side of the widow, seized me by the throat and demanded how the devil I came there?

My wits had not entirely deserted me, and I managed to tell quite a plausible story. I candidly confessed that I had been to the theatre and stated that I had got into the house through the kitchen window. Of course I said nothing about Anderson and Mrs. Romaine.

"You have been drinking," said Mr. Romaine, in a tone that was by no means severe, "but I forgive you for that, and also for having disobeyed me by going to the theatre. Be a good boy in future, and you shall never want a friend while I live."

While he was speaking, I looked about the room. It was exquisitely furnished with the most refined and elegant taste. Mrs. Raymond, who still sat upon the sofa, blushed deeply as her eyes encountered mine. She was *en deshabille*, and looked charming. I could not help admiring the divine perfections of her form, as *revealed* by the deliciously careless attire which she wore. I did not wonder that my respected presence confused her, for she had always held herself up as the very pink and pattern of female propriety, and besides, she often lectured me severely upon the enormity of some of my juvenile offences, which came to her knowledge.

Mr. Romaine continued to address me, thus:

"If you will solemnly promise to say nothing about having seen me in this room, I will reward you handsomely."

I readily gave the required promise, whereupon my pious employer presented me with a five-dollar bill, which I received with all the nonchalance in the world. I then withdrew, and reached my own room without encountering any more adventures. Sleep did not visit me that night, for my thoughts were too busily engaged with the discoveries which I had made; and besides, the blissful consciousness of being the possessor of the princely sum of fifteen dollars, would have kept me awake, independent of anything else.

A day or two after these occurrences, while looking over one of the morning newspapers, I saw an advertisement signed by my uncle, in which that worthy man offered a reward for my apprehension. The notice contained a minute description of my personal appearance and the clothes which I had on when I "ran away." Although my garments had been entirely changed, I was fearful that some one might recognize my person, and carry me back to my uncle's house, where I had every reason to expect far worse treatment than I had ever received before. But Mr. Romaine, to whom I showed the advertisement, told me not to be at all alarmed, as he would protect me at any risk. This assurance made me feel much easier. I was never molested in consequence of that advertisement.

After the night on which I had detected the intrigue of my employer and his wife, I began to live emphatically "in clover," and accumulated money tolerably fast. All the parties concerned treated me with the utmost consideration and respect. Mr. Romaine suffered me to do pretty much as I pleased in the printing office, and so I enjoyed a very agreeable and leisurely time of it, doing as much Sunday printing on my own account as I desired, and going to the theatre as often as I wished. Mr. Anderson would occasionally slip a five dollar note into my hand, at the same time enjoining me to "keep mum;" Mrs. Romaine, with her own fair hands, made me a dozen superb shirts, supplied me with handkerchiefs, stockings and fancy cravats innumerable, and so arranged it that when I returned from the theatre at night, a nice little supper awaited me in the kitchen. These repasts she would sometimes share with me, for, like a sensible woman, she was fond of all the good things of this life, including good eating and drinking. Anderson would join us occasionally, and a snug, cosy little party we made. Mrs. Raymond, the pretty widow, was not backward in testifying to me how grateful she was for my silence with reference to her frailty. She made me frequent presents of money, and gave me an elegant and valuable ring, which I wore until the "intervention of unfortunate circumstance" compelled me to consign it to the custody of "my uncle"—not my beloved relative of Thomas street, (peace to his memory, for he has gone the way of all pork,)—but that accommodating uncle of mine and everybody else, Mr. Simpson, who dwelleth in the *Rue de Chatham*, and whose mansion is decorated with three gilded balls. Kind, convenient Uncle Simpson!

Ah! those were my halcyon days, when not a single care cast its shadow o'er my soul. As I think of that season of unalloyed happiness, I involuntarily exclaim, in the words of a fine popular song—

"I would I were a boy again!"

Three years passed away, unmarked by the occurrence of any event of sufficient importance to merit a place in this narrative. When I reached my fifteenth year, the fashionable boarding-house of Mrs. Romaine became the scene of a tragedy so bloody, so awful and so appalling, that even now, while I think and write about it, my blood runs cold in my veins. That terrible affair can no more be obliterated from my memory than can the sun be effaced from the arch of heaven; and to my dying day, its recollection will continue to haunt me like a hideous spectre.

But I must devote a separate chapter to the details of that sanguinary event. I would gladly escape from the task of describing it; but, of course, were I to omit it, this narrative would be incomplete. Therefore the unwelcome duty must be performed.

---

# CHAPTER III

***In which is enacted a bloody tragedy.***

I began to observe with considerable uneasiness, that Mr. Romaine stealthily regarded his wife with looks of intense hatred and malignant ferocity; then he would transfer his gaze from her to Mr. Anderson, who was altogether unconscious of the scrutiny. My employer was usually a very quiet man, but I knew that his passions were very violent, and that, when once thoroughly aroused, he was capable of perpetrating almost any act of savage vengeance. I began to fear that he suspected the intimacy which existed between his adulterous wife and her paramour. By the way it may be as well to remark that I had never told either Anderson or Mrs. Romaine of the intrigue between Mr. Romaine and the widow, Mrs. Raymond; and it is scarcely necessary to observe that I was equally discreet in withholding from my employer and his "ladye love" all knowledge of the state of affairs between the other parties.

I communicated my fears to Mr. Anderson, but he laughed at them saying—

"Nonsense, my dear boy—why should Romaine suspect anything of the kind? I and Harriet (Mrs. Romaine) have always been very discreet and careful. Our intimacy began three or four years ago; and as it has lasted that length of time without discovery, it is scarcely likely to be detected *now*. You are quite sure that you have given Romaine no hint of the affair?"

"Do you think me capable of such base treachery?" I demanded, with an offended air.

"Forgive me," said Anderson, "I did wrong to doubt you. Believe me, your fears are groundless; however, I thank you for the caution, and shall hereafter exercise additional care, so as to prevent the possibility of discovery. Here is a ticket for the opera to-night; when you return, which will be about midnight, come to Harriet's room, and we three will sup like two kings and a queen."

Having dressed myself with unusual care, I went to the opera. While listening to the divine strains of a celebrated *prima donna*, my attention was attracted by a group occupying one of the most conspicuous boxes. This group consisted of a youth apparently about my own age, and two showy looking females whose dresses were cut so low as to reveal much more of their busts than decency could sanction, even among an opera audience. There could be no doubt as to the character of these two women. I examined their youthful cavalier with attention; and soon recognized my *quondum* friend and pitcher —JACK SLACK. Jack was magnificently dressed, and his appearance was truly superb. The most fastidious Parisian exquisite—even the great Count D'Orsay himself might have envied him the arrangement of his hair, the tie of his cravat, the spotlessness of his white kids. He flourished a glittering, jeweled *lorgnette*, and the way the fellow put on "French airs" must have been a caution to the proudest scion of aristocracy in the house.

After a little while Jack saw me; and, having taken a good long stare at me through his opera-glass, he beckoned me to come to him, at the same time pointing significantly at one of his "lady" companions, as if to intimate that she was entirely at my disposal. But I shook my head, and did not stir, for I had no desire to resume my acquaintance with that fascinating but mysterious youth. Perhaps I entertained a presentiment that he was destined to become, to both of us, the cause of a great misfortune.

Jack looked angry and disappointed, at my refusal to accept of his hospitable invitation. He directed the attention of his women towards me, and I saw that they were attempting to titter and sneer at my expense;—but the effort was a total failure, for there was not a better-dressed person in the house than I was. Having honored the envious party with a smile of scorn,—which, I flattered myself, was perfectly successful,—I turned towards the stage, and did not indulge in another look at Jack or his friends during the remainder of the opera. I am convinced that from that hour, Jack Slack became my mortal foe.

At the conclusion of the performances, I left the house and saw Jack getting into a carriage with the two courtezans. He observed me, and uttered a decisive shout, to which I paid no attention, but hurried home, anxious to make one of the little party in the apartment of Mrs. Romaine, and quite ready to partake of the delicacies which, I knew, would be provided.

On my arrival home, I immediately repaired to Mrs. Romaine's private room, where I found that good lady in company with Mr. Anderson. We three sat down to supper in the highest possible spirits. Alas! how little did we anticipate the terrible catastrophe that was so soon to follow!

The more substantial portion of the banquet having been disposed of, the sparkling wine-cup was circulated freely, and we became very gay and jovial. Unrestrained by my presence, and exhilarated by the rosy beverage of jolly Bacchus, the lovers indulged in many little acts of tender dalliance. Always making it a point to mind my own business, I applied myself diligently to the bottle, for the wine was excellent and the sardines had made me thirsty. I had just lighted a cigar, and was resigning myself to the luxurious and deliciously soothing influence of the weed, when the door was thrown violently open, and Mr. Romaine rushed into the room.

His appearance was frightful! his face was dreadfully pale, and his eyes glared with the combined fires of jealousy and rage. Intense excitement caused him to quiver in every limb. In one hand he grasped a pistol, and in the other a bowie knife of the largest and most formidable kind.

It was but too evident that my fears had been well founded, and that Mr. Romaine had discovered the intimacy between Anderson and his wife.

The reader will agree with me that the "injured husband" was equally culpable on account of his intrigue with the young and handsome widow, Mrs. Raymond.—How prone are many people to lose sight of their own imperfections while they censure and severely punish the failings of those who are not a whit more guilty than themselves! The swinish glutton condemns the drunkard—the villainous seducer reproves the frequenter of brothels—the arch hypocrite takes to task the open, undisguised sinner—and the rich, miserly old reprobate, whose wealth places him above the possibility of ever coming to want, who would sooner "hang the guiltless than eat his mutton cold," and who would not bestow a cent upon a poor devil to keep him from starving—that old rascal, perhaps, in his capacity as a magistrate, sentences to jail an unfortunate man whom hunger has driven into the "crime" of stealing a loaf of bread! Bah! ladies and gentlemen, take the *beams* out of your own eyes before you allude to the *motes* in the optics of your fellow beings. That's *my* advice, free of charge.

On seeing her husband enter in that furious and threatening manner, Mrs. Romaine, overcome with fear and shame—for she well knew that her guilt had been detected—fell to the floor insensible. Anderson, confused and not knowing what to say, sat motionless as a statue;—while I awaited, with almost trembling anxiety, the issue of this most extraordinary state of affairs.

Romaine was the first to break the silence, and he spoke in a tone of voice that was singularly calm considering his physical agitation.

"Well, sir," said he, addressing Anderson—"you are enjoying yourself finely —drinking my wine, devouring my provisions, and making love to my wife in her own bed-chamber. Anderson, for some time past I have suspected you and Harriet of being guilty of criminal intimacy. I have noticed your secret signs, and have read and interpreted the language of your eyes, whenever you and she have exchanged glances in my presence. You both took me to be a weak fool, too blind and imbecile to detect your adulterous intercourse; but I have now come to convince you that I am a man capable of avenging his ruined conjugal honor!"

Anderson, recovering some degree of his usual self-possession, remarked,

"Your accusation, sir, is unjust. Your wife and myself are friends, and nothing more. She invited me to sup with her here to-night and that is all about it. If our intentions were criminal, would we have courted the presence of a third party?"

With these words, Anderson pointed towards me, but Romaine, without observing me at all, continued to address the paramour of his wife.

"Anderson, you are a liar, and the falsehoods which you have uttered, only serve to increase your guilt, and confirm me in my resolution to sacrifice both you and that guilty woman who lies yonder. Can I disbelieve the evidence of my own eyes? Must I go into particulars, and say that last night, at about this hour, in the kitchen—ha! you turn pale—you tremble—your guilt is confessed. I would have killed you last night, Anderson, but I had not the weapons. This knife and pistol I purchased to-day, *and I shall use them*!

"Try and revive that *harlot*, for I would speak with her ere she dies!"

Anderson mechanically obeyed. Placing the insensible form of Mrs. Romaine upon a sofa, he sprinkled water upon her face, and she was soon restored to a state of consciousness. For a few moments she gazed about her wildly; and then, when her eyes settled upon her husband, and she saw the terrible weapons with which he was armed, she covered her face with her hands and trembled in an agony of terror, for she knew that her life was in the greatest possible danger.

Romaine now addressed his wife in a tone of calmness which was, under the circumstances, far more terrible than the most violent outburst of passion:

"Harriet," said he—"I now fully comprehend your reasons for requesting to be allowed to occupy a separate apartment. You desired an opportunity to gratify your licentious propensities without any restraint. Woman, why have you used me thus? Have I deserved this infamous treatment? Have I ever used you unkindly, or spoken a harsh word to you? Do you think that I will tamely wear the horns which you and your paramour have planted upon my brow? Do you think that I will suffer myself to be made an object of scorn, and allow myself to be pointed at and ridiculed by a sneering community?"

"Forgive me," murmured the unhappy wife—"I will not offend again. I acknowledge that I have committed a grievous sin; but Heaven only knows how sincerely I repent of it!"

"Your repentance comes too late," said Romaine, hoarsely—"Heaven may forgive you, but *I* shall not! You say that you will not offend again. Having forever destroyed my happiness, my peace of mind, and my honor, *you will not offend again*! You shall not have the opportunity, wretched woman. You shall no longer survive your infamy. You and the partner of your guilt must die!"

With these words, Romaine cocked his pistol and approached his wife, saying, in a low, savage tone that evinced the desperate purpose of his heart—

"Take your choice, madam; do you prefer to die by *lead* or by *steel*?"

The miserable woman threw herself upon her knees, exclaiming—

"Mercy, husband—mercy! Do not kill me, for I am not prepared to die!"

"You call me husband *now*—you, who have so long refused to receive me as a husband. Come—I am impatient to shed your blood, and that of your paramour. Breathe a short prayer to Heaven, for mercy and forgiveness, and then resign your body to death and your soul to eternity!"

So saying the desperate and half-crazy man raised on high the glittering knife. Poor Mrs. Romaine uttered a shriek, and, before she could repeat it, the knife descended with the swiftness of lightning, and penetrated her heart. Her blood spouted all over her white dress, and she sank down at the murderer's feet, a lifeless corpse!

Paralyzed with horror, I could neither move nor speak. Anderson also stood motionless, like a bird which is subjected to the fascinating gaze of a serpent. Notwithstanding the terrible danger in which he was placed, he seemed to be rooted to the spot and incapable of making a single effort to save himself by either resistance or flight.

The scene was most extraordinary, thrilling and awful. The luxurious chamber —the failing lamp—the murderer, holding in his hand the bloody knife—the doomed Anderson, whose soul was quivering on the brink of the dread abyss of eternity; all these combined to form a spectacle of the most strange and appalling character.

Romaine now raised his pistol and took deliberate aim at Anderson, saying,

"My work is but half done; it is *your* turn now! Are you ready?"

"Do not shoot me like a dog," implored the unfortunate young man, who, to do him justice, possessed a considerable amount of courage—"give me, at least, *some* chance for my life. If I have wronged you, and I candidly confess that I have, I am ready to give you the satisfaction of a gentleman. Give me a pistol, place me upon an equal footing with yourself, and we will settle the matter as becomes men of honor. This boy, here, will be a witness of the affair."

To this proposition, Romaine scornfully replied,

"I admire your assurance, sir.—After seducing the wife, you want a chance to shoot the husband. Well, as I am an accommodating man, it shall be as you say, for I am sick of life and care not if I am killed. But I have no other pistol. Stay!—suppose we *toss up* a coin, and thus decide which of us shall have this weapon, with the privilege of using it. Here is a quarter of a dollar; I will throw it up in the air, and when it falls upon the floor, if the *head* is uppermost, the pistol is *mine*; but if the *tail* is uppermost, the pistol shall be *yours*. I warn you that if I win, I shall show you no mercy; and, if you win, I shall expect none from you. Do you agree to this?"

"I do," replied Anderson, firmly, "and I thank you for your fairness."

Romaine threw up the coin, which spun around in the air and landed upon the carpet. How strange that it should have become the province of that insignificant coin to decide which of those two men must die!

Romaine calmly took the dim lamp from the table, and knelt down upon the carpet in a pool of his wife's blood.

"Watch me closely, and see that I do not touch the coin," said he, as he bent eagerly over the life-deciding quarter of a dollar.

How my heart beat at that moment, and what must have been the sensation of poor Anderson!

"*The head is uppermost, and I have won!*" said Romaine, in a hoarse whisper —"come and see for yourself."

"I am satisfied, your word is sufficient," said Anderson, with a shudder, as he folded his arms across his breast and seemed to abandon himself to profound despair.

Romaine's pale face assumed an expression of savage delight, as he raised the pistol and pointed it at the head of his intended victim, saying—

"Then, sir, nothing remains but for me to avail myself of the favor which fortune has conferred upon me. Young man, in five seconds I shall fire!"

"Hold!" cried Anderson, "I have a favor to ask, which I am sure you will not refuse to grant me. Before I die, let me write a couple of letters, and make a few notes of the manner in which I wish my property to be disposed of. It is the last request of a dying man."

"It is granted," said Romaine, "there, upon that *escritoire*, are writing materials. But make haste, for I am impatient to finish this disagreeable business."

Anderson sat down, and began to write rapidly. I longed to rush out and give the alarm, so that the impending tragedy might be averted; but I feared that any movement on my part might result in the passage of a bullet through my brain, and therefore I remained quiet, for which I am sure, no sensible reader will blame me.

Poor Anderson! tears gushed from his eyes and streamed down his cheeks while he was writing one of the letters, which, as I afterwards ascertained, was addressed to a young lady to whom he was engaged to be married. He wrote two letters, folded, sealed and directed them; these he handed to me, saying—

"Have the kindness to deliver these letters to the persons to whom they are addressed. Will you faithfully promise to do this?"

I promised, of course; he shook hands with me, and bade me farewell; then, calmly turning towards Romaine, he announced his readiness to die. Up to that moment, I had tried to persuade myself that Anderson's life would be spared, thinking that Romaine must have had enough of blood after slaying his wife in that barbarous manner. But I was doomed to be terribly disappointed. Scarcely had Anderson muttered the words, "I am ready to die," when Romaine pulled the trigger of the upraised pistol, and the young merchant fell dead upon the floor, the bullet having penetrated his brain.

"Now I am satisfied, for I have had my revenge," said the murderer, coolly, as he wiped the perspiration from his pallid brow.

"Blood-thirsty villain!" exclaimed I, unable longer to restrain my indignation —"you will swing upon the gallows for this night's work!"

"Not so," rejoined Romaine, calmly, "for I do not intend to survive this wholesale butchery, and did not, from the first. I was determined that Anderson should die, at all events. *He won the pistol*, for the coin fell with the tail uppermost. Had he stooped to examine it, I would have blown out his brains, just the same. But hark! the boarders and inmates of the house have been aroused by the report of the pistol, and they are hastening here. The gallows— no, no, I must avoid *that*! They shall not take me alive. Now, may heaven have mercy upon my guilty soul!"

With these words the unhappy man seized the Bowie knife and plunged it into his heart, thus adding the crime of suicide to the two atrocious murders which he had just committed.

Scarcely had this crowning point of the fearful tragedy been enacted, when a crowd of people, half-dressed and excited, rushed into the room. Among them was the beautiful widow, Mrs. Raymond. On seeing the bleeding corpse of Romaine stretched upon the floor, she gave utterance to a piercing scream and fell down insensible.

In the horror and confusion that prevailed, I was unnoticed. I determined to leave the house, never to return, for I dreaded being brought before the public, as a witness, being a great hater of notoriety in any shape. (The reader may smile at this last remark; but I assure him, or her, that my frequent appearance before the public as a writer, has been the result of necessity—not of inclination.)

Accordingly, I left the house unobserved, and took lodgings for the remainder of the night at a hotel. But sleep visited me not, for my mind was too deeply engrossed with the bloody scenes which I had witnessed, to suffer the approach of "tired nature's sweet restorer." In the morning I arose early, and investigated the condition of my finances. The result of this examination was highly satisfactory, for I found that I was the possessor of a considerable sum of money.

I walked about the city until noon, uncertain how to act. I felt a strong disposition to travel, and see the world;—but I could not make up my mind in what direction to go. After a sumptuous dinner at Sandy Welch's "Terrapin Lunch,"—one of the most famous *restaurants* of the day—I indulged in a contemplative walk up Broadway. Such thoughts as these ran through my mind:—"I cannot help contrasting my present situation with the position I was in, three years ago. Then I was almost penniless, and gladly breakfasted on dry bread at a street pump; now I have three hundred dollars in my pocket, and have just dined like an epicurean prince. Then I was clad in garments that were coarse and cheap; now I am dressed in the finest raiment that money could procure. Then I had no trade; now I have a profession which will be to me an unfailing means of support. But, alas! then I was comparatively innocent, and ignorant of the wicked ways of the world; now, although only fifteen years of age, I am too thoroughly posted up on all the mysteries ofcity follies and vices. No matter: there's nothing like experience, afterall."

Comforting myself with this philosophical reflection, I strolled on. A newsboy came along, bawling out, at the top of his voice—"Here's the extra *Sun*, with a full account of the two murders and suicide in William street last night—only one cent!" Of course I purchased a copy; and, upon perusing the account, I could not help smiling at the ludicrous and absurd exaggerations which it contained. It was a perfect modern tragedy of *Othello*, with Romaine as the Moor, Mrs. Romaine as Desdemona, and Anderson as a sort of cross between Iago and Michael Cassio. I was not alluded to in any way whatever, which caused me to rejoice exceedingly.[D]

Suddenly remembering the two letters which had been confided to my care by the unfortunate Anderson, I resolved to deliver them immediately. One was directed to a Mr. Sargent, in Pine street. I soon found the place, which was a large mercantile establishment. Over the door was the sign "*Anderson & Sargent.*" This had been poor Anderson's place of business, and Sargent had been his partner. I entered, found Mr. Sargent in the counting-room, and delivered to him the letter. He opened it, read it through coolly, shrugged his shoulders, and said—

"I have already been made acquainted with the full particulars of this melancholy affair. Anderson was a clever fellow, and I'm sorry he's gone, although his death will certainly promote my interests. He gives me, in this letter, every necessary instruction as to the disposition of his property, and he also directs me to present you with the sum of two hundred dollars, both as an acknowledgement of your services and as a token of his friendship. I will fill out a check for the amount immediately."

This instance of Anderson's kindness and generosity, almost at the very moment of his death, deeply affected me; and, at the same time, I could not help feeling disgusted with the heartlessness displayed by Sargent, who regarded the tragical death of his partner merely as an event calculated to advance his own interests.

Having received the check, I withdrew from the august presence of Mr. Sargent, who was a tall, thin, hook-nosed personage, of unwholesome aspect and abrupt manners. I drew the money at the bank, and then hastened to deliver the other letter, which was addressed to Miss Grace Arlington, whose residence was designated as being situated in one of the fashionable squares up-town. I had no difficulty in finding the house, which was of the most elegant and aristocratic appearance. My appeal to the doorbell was responded to by a smart-looking female domestic, who, on learning my errand, ushered me into the presence of her mistress. Miss Grace Arlington was a very lovely and delicate young lady, whose soft eyes beamed with tenderness and sensibility, whose voice was as sweet as the music of an angel's harp, while her step was as light as the tread of a fairy whose tiny feet will not crush the leaves of a rose. When I handed her the letter, and she recognized the well known handwriting, she bestowed upon me a winning and grateful smile which I shall never forget. My heart misgave me as she opened the missive, for I could well divine its contents; and I almost reproached myself for being the messenger of such evil tidings. I watched her closely as she read. She was naturally somewhat pale, but I saw her face grow ghastly white before she had read two lines. When she had finished the perusal of the fatal letter, she pressed her hand upon her breast, murmured "Oh God!" and would have fallen to the floor if I had not caught her in my arms.

"Curses on my stupidity!" I muttered, as I placed her insensible form upon a sofa—"I ought to have prepared her gradually for the terrible announcement which I knew that letter to contain!"

I rang the bell furiously, and the almost deafening summons was answered by half-a-dozen female servants, who, on seeing the condition of their young Mistress, set up a loud chorus of screams. The uproar brought Mr. Arlington, the father of the young lady, to the scene. He was a fine-looking old gentleman, a retired merchant and a *millionaire*. I hastened to explain to him all that had occurred, and Anderson's letter, which lay upon the floor, confirmed my statements. Mr. Arlington was horror-struck, for he, as well as his daughter, had until that moment been in happy ignorance of the bloody affair. The old gentleman had first established Anderson in business, and he had always cherished for that unfortunate young man the warmest friendship. No wonder, then, that he was overpowered when he became aware of the tragical end of him whom he had expected so shortly to become his son-in- law.

A celebrated physician, who resided next door, was sent for. He happened to be at home, and arrived almost instantly. He knelt down beside the broken-hearted girl, and, as his fingers touched her wrist, a look of profound grief settled upon his benevolent face.

"Well, Doctor," exclaimed Mr. Arlington, breathlessly, "what is the matter with my child? She will recover soon, will she not? It is merely a fainting fit produced by the reception of unwelcome news."

"Alas, sir!" replied the Doctor, in a tone of deep sympathy, as he brushed away the tears from his eyes—"I may as well tell you the melancholy truth at once. The sudden shock caused by the unwelcome news you speak of, has proved fatal; your daughter is dead!"

Poor old Arlington staggered to a seat, covered his face with his hands, and moaned in the agony of his spirits. Notwithstanding all his wealth, how I pitied him!

Seeing that I could be of no service whatever, I left the house of mourning and walked down town in a very thoughtful mood. I had already begun to enter upon an experience such as few youths of fifteen are ever called upon to encounter; and I wondered what the dim, uncertain Future had in store for me.

However, as the reader will see in the next chapter, I did not long suffer my mind to be intruded upon by melancholy reflections.

## FOOTNOTES:

[D] Many of my New York readers will remember the "William Street Tragedy," to which I have alluded. The bloody event created the most intense excitement at the time of its occurrence. Having witnessed the horrible affair, I have truly related all the facts concerning it.

---

# CHAPTER IV

***In which I set forth upon my travels, and met with a great misfortune.***

Having plenty of means at my disposal, I determined to enjoy myself to the full extent of my physical and intellectual capacity, for I remembered the graceful words of the charming poet who sung—

> "Go it while you're young:
> For, when you get old, you can't!"

Behold me, at the age of fifteen, fairly launched upon all the dissipations of a corrupt and licentious city! It is not without a feeling of shame that I make these confessions; but truth compels me to do so. I soon became thoroughly initiated into all the mysteries of high and low life in New York. In my daily and nightly peregrinations I frequently encountered my old friend Jack Slack; we never spoke, but on the contrary regarded each other with looks of enmity and defiance. Stronger and stronger within me grew the presentiment that this mysterious youth was destined to become my evil genius and the cause of a great misfortune. Therefore, whenever I met him, I could not help shuddering with dread.

Three years passed away in this manner, and I had reached the age of eighteen, with an unimpaired constitution and a firm belief that I was destined to exist for ever. I had lived luxuriously upon the earnings of my pen, for I was a regular contributor to the Knickerbroker Magazine and other popular periodicals. Having accumulated considerable money, notwithstanding my extravagance, I resolved to take a Southern tour, visiting Philadelphia, Washington, and other cities of note. Accordingly, one fine day, I found myself established in comfortable quarters, at the most fashionable hotel in the "city of brotherly love." I became a regular frequenter of the theatres and other places of amusement, and formed the acquaintance of many actors and literary people. It was here that I had the honor of being introduced to Booth, the great tragedian, now dead; to "Ned Forrest," the American favorite; to "Uncle" J.R. Scott, as fine a man as ever drank a noggin of ale or ate a "dozen raw," and to Major Richardson, the author of "Wacousta," and the "Monk Knight of St. John," the latter being one of the most voluptuous works ever written. Poor Major! his was a melancholy end. He was formerly a Major in the British army, and was a gentleman by birth, education and principle. Possessing a fine person, a generous heart and the most winning manners, he was a general favorite with his associates. He became the victim of rapacious publishers, and grew poor. Too proud to accept of assistance from his friends, he retired to obscure lodgings and there endeavored to support himself by the productions of his pen. But his spirit was broken and his intellect crushed by the base ingratitude of those who should have been his warmest friends. Often have I visited him in his garret—for he actually occupied one; and, with a bottle of whiskey before us, we have condemned the world as being full of selfishness, ingratitude and villainy. Winter came on, and the Major had no fuel, nor the means of procuring any. I have repeatedly called upon him and found him sitting in the intensely cold atmosphere of his miserable apartment, wrapped in a blanket and busily engaged in writing with a hand that was blue and trembled with the cold. He firmly refused to receive aid, in any shape, from his friends; and they were obliged to witness his gradual decay with sad hearts. The gallant Major always persisted in denying that he needed anything; he swore his garret was the most comfortable place in the world, and that the introduction of a fire would have been preposterous; he always affirmed with a round military oath, that he "lived like a fighting-cock," and was never without his bottle of wine at dinner; yet I once came upon him rather unexpectedly, and found him dining upon a crust of bread and a red herring. Sometimes, but rarely, he appeared at the theatres, and, upon such occasions, he was always scrupulously well-dressed, for Major Richardson would never appear abroad otherwise than as a gentleman. Want, privation and disappointment finally conquered him; he grew thin, and haggard, and melancholy, and reserved, and discouraged the visits of his friends who used to love to assemble at his humble lodgings and avail themselves of his splendid conversational powers, or listen to his personal reminiscences and racy anecdotes of military life. One morning he was found dead in his bed; and his death caused the most profound grief in the breasts of all who knew him as he deserved to be known, and who respected him for his many excellent qualities of head and heart. His remains received a handsome and appropriate burial; and many a tear was shed o'er the grave of him who had been a gallant soldier and a celebrated author, but a truly wronged and most unfortunate man.

The reader will, I am sure, pardon this digression, for I was anxious to do justice to the memory of a much-valued friend and literary brother. I now resume the direct course of my narrative, and come to the darkest portion of my career.

One night, in a billiard room, I had a very unpleasant encounter with an old acquaintance. I observed, at one of the tables, a young man whose countenance seemed strangely familiar to me, although I did not immediately recognize him. He was dressed in the extreme of fashion, and his upper lip was darkened by an incipient moustache—the result, doubtless, of many months of industrious cultivation. A cigar was in his mouth, and a billiard-cue was in his hand; and he profusely adorned his conversation with the most extravagant oaths. Altogether, he seemed to be a very "fast" young man; and I puzzled my brain in endeavoring to remember where I had met him before.

Suddenly, he raised his eyes, and their gaze encountered mine; then I wondered that I had not before recognized "my old friend," Jack Slack!

"This fellow is my evil genius; he follows me everywhere," thought I, turning to leave the saloon. Would to heaven that I had never entered it! But regrets are useless now.

Jack stepped after me, and detained me. I instantly saw that trouble was about to come.

"Greenhorn," said Jack, with an air of angry reproach, as he laid his hand upon my shoulder—"why do you so continually avoid me? What in the devil's name have I ever done to deserve this treatment? Have I ever injured you in any way? Damn it, we are equal in age, and in disposition—let us be friends. I can put you in a way, in this city, to enjoy the tallest kind of sport. Give me your hand, and let's go up to the bar and take a social drink."

"Jack," said I, seriously and very calmly—"I will shake hands with you in friendship, but I candidly confess that I do not like you; and I believe that it will be better for us both not to associate together at all. Observe me!—I have no hard feelings against you;—you are a clever fellow, and generous to a fault; but something whispers to me that we must not be companions, and I therefore respectfully desire you not to speak to me again. Good night."[E]

I turned to go, but Jack placed himself directly in my path, and said, in a voice that was hoarse with passion—

"Stay and hear me. We must not part in this way. Do you think that I will tamely submit to be *cut* in a manner so disgraceful? Do you think that I am going to remain the object of an unfounded and ridiculous prejudice? Explain yourself, and apologize, or by G——, it will be the worse for you!"

"Explain myself—apologize!" I scornfully repeated—"you are a fool, and don't know to whom you are talking. Let me go."

"No!" passionately screamed my enraged antagonist, who was somewhat intoxicated—"you must stay and hear me out. I may as well throw off the mask at once. Know, then, that I hate you like hell-fire, and that, the very first time I saw you, I resolved to make you as bad as myself. Therefore did I induce you to drink, and visit disreputable places. The cool contempt with which you have always treated me, had increased my hatred ten-fold. I thirst for vengeance, and *I'll fix you yet*!"

"Do your worst," said I, contemptuously; and again did I essay to take my departure. Meanwhile, during the quarrel, the frequents of the saloon had gathered around and appeared to enjoy the scene highly.

"If he has given you any cause of offence, Jack, why don't you pitch into him?" suggested a half-drunken fellow who bore the enviable reputation of being a most expert pickpocket.

Jack unfortunately adopted the suggestion, and struck me with all his force. I of course returned the blow, with very tolerable effect.—Had the row commenced and terminated in mere *fisticuffs* all would have been well, and I should not now be called upon to write down the details of a bloody tragedy.

Drawing a dirk-knife from his breast, Jack attacked me with the utmost fury. I then did what any other person, situated as I was, would have done—I acted in my own defence. "Self-defence" is universally acknowledged to be the "first law of nature." There was I, a stranger, savagely attacked by a young man armed with a dangerous weapon, and surrounded by his friends and associates—a desperate set, who seemed disposed to assist in the task of demolishing me.

I quickly drew from my pocket a pistol, without which, at that time, I never travelled. Before, however, I could cock and level it, my infuriated enemy dashed his dirk-knife into my face, and the point entered my right eye. It was fortunate that the weapon did not penetrate the brain, and cause my instant death.

Maddened by the horrible pain which I suffered, and believing myself to be mortally wounded, I raised the pistol and discharged it. Jack Slack fell to the floor, a corpse, his head being shattered to pieces. *I never regretted the act.*

A cry of horror and dismay burst from the lips of all present, on witnessing this dreadful but justifiable deed of retribution.

"Gentlemen," said I, as the blood was trickling down my face—"I call upon you all to witness that I slew this young man in self-defence. He drove me to commit the deed, and I could not avoid it. I am willing and anxious to abide the decision of a jury of my countrymen; therefore, send for an officer, and I will voluntarily surrender myself into his custody."

Scarcely had I uttered these words, when the excruciating torment which I suffered caused me to faint away. When I recovered, I found myself in a prison-cell, with a bandage over my damaged optic, and a physician feeling my pulse.

"Ah!" said I, looking around, "I am in *limbo*, I see. Well, I do not fear the result. But, doctor, am I seriously injured—am I likely to kick the bucket?"

"Not at all," was the doctor's encouraging reply—"but you have lost the sight of your eye."

"Oh, is *that* all?" said I with a laugh—"well, I believe that it is said in the Bible somewhere, that it is better to enter the kingdom of heaven with one eye than to go to the devil with two."

The physician departed for his home, and I departed for the land of dreams. The pain of my wound had considerably mitigated, and I slept quite comfortably.

I have always been somewhat of a philosopher in the way of enduring the ills of life, and I tried to reconcile myself to my misfortune and situation with as good a grace as possible. In this I succeeded much better than might have been expected. When a person loses an eye and is at the same time imprisoned for killing another individual, it is certainly natural for that unfortunate person to yield to despair; but, seeing the uselessness of grief, I resolved to "face the music" with all the courage of which I was possessed.

Two or three days passed away, and I became almost well—for, to use a common expression, I owned the constitution of a horse. The newspapers which I was allowed to send out and purchase, made me acquainted with something that rather surprised me, for they communicated to me the information that Jack Slack, the young gentleman to whom I had presented a ticket of admission to the other world, was a person whose *real* name was John Shaffer, *alias* Slippery Jack, *alias* Jack Slack. His profession was that of a pickpocket, in which avocation he had always been singularly expert. He was well known to the police, and had been frequently imprisoned. I was gratified to see that the newspapers all justified me in what I had done, and predicted my honorable discharge from custody. That prediction proved correct; for, after I had been in confinement a week, the Grand Jury failed to bring a bill of indictment against me, and I was consequently set at liberty.

Tired of Philadelphia, I went to Washington. A New York member of Congress, with whom I was well acquainted, volunteered to show me the "lions;" and I had the honor of a personal introduction to Mr. Van Buren and other distinguished official personages. Some people would be surprised if they did but know of the splendid dissipation that prevails among the "dignitaries of the nation" at Washington.

I have seen more than one member of the United States Senate staggering through the streets, from what cause the reader will have no difficulty in judging. I have seen a great statesman, since deceased, carried from an after-dinner table to his chamber. I have seen the honorable Secretary of one of the National departments engaged in a brawl in a brothel. I have seen

Representatives fighting in a bar-room like so many rowdies, and I have heard them use language that would disgrace a beggar in his drink. I need not allude to the many outrageous scenes which have been enacted in the councils of the nation; for the newspapers have already given them sufficient publicity.

Leaving Washington, I journeyed South, and, after many adventures which the limits of this work will not permit me to describe, I arrived in the City of New Orleans. I had no difficulty in procuring a lucrative situation as reporter on a popular daily newspaper; and enjoyed free access to all the theatres and other places of amusement.—I remained in New Orleans just one year; but, not liking the climate,—and finding, moreover, that I was living too "*fast*," and accumulating no money,—I resolved to "pull up stakes" and start in a Northerly direction. Accordingly, I returned to Philadelphia.

It would have been much better for me had I remained in New Orleans, for the hardest kind of times prevailed in the "Quaker City," on my arrival there. It was almost impossible to obtain employment of any description; and many actors, authors and artists, as well as mechanics, were most confoundedly "hard up." I soon exhausted the contents of my purse; and, like the Prodigal Son, "began to be in want."

One fine day, in a very disconsolate mood, I was wandering through an obscure street, when I encountered a former lady acquaintance, whom, I trust, the reader has not forgotten.

But the particulars of that unexpected encounter, and the details of what subsequently transpired, are worthy of a separate chapter.

## FOOTNOTES:

[E] It is singular, but it is true, that a few nights prior to the tragical occurrences which I am about to relate, I saw, in a dream, a perfect and exact fore-shadow of the whole melancholy affair! Who can explain this mystery?

---

# CHAPTER V

***I encountered a lady acquaintance, and, like a knight errant of old, became the champion of beauty.***

A musical voice pronounced my name; and looking up, I saw a very handsome woman seated at the window of a rather humble wooden tenement, the first floor of which was occupied as a cheap grocery. I immediately recognised my old acquaintance, Mrs. Raymond, the pretty widow of the fashionable boarding-house in William street, New York—she who had carried on an intrigue with Mr. Romaine. I have, in a former chapter, described the terrible affair in which Romaine slew his wife and Anderson her paramour—and then killed himself.

I need scarcely say that this encounter with Mrs. Raymond, under such peculiar circumstances, rather astonished me. I had known her as a lady of wealth, and the most elegant and fastidious tastes; and yet here I found her living in an obscure and disreputable portion of the city, and occupying a house which none but the victims of poverty would ever have consented to dwell in.

"Wait until I come down and conduct you up stairs," said Mrs. Raymond; and she disappeared from the window.

In a few moments she opened the door leading to the upper part of the house; and having warmly shaken hands with me, she desired me to follow her. I complied, and was shown into an apartment on the second floor.

"This is my room, and my only one; don't laugh at it," said Mrs. Raymond, with a melancholy smile.

I looked around me. The room was small, but scrupulously clean; and, notwithstanding the scantiness and humility of the furniture, a certain air of refinement prevailed. I have often remarked that it is impossible for a person who has been accustomed to the elegancies of life, to become so low, in fortune or character, as to entirely lose every trace of former superiority.

> "You may break, you may ruin the vase, if you will,
> But the scent of the roses will cling 'round it still!"

Mrs. Raymond's apartment merely contained a fine table, two or three common chairs, a closet, a bed, and a harp—the relic of better and happier days. The uncarpeted floor was almost as white as snow—and certainly no snow could be purer or whiter than the drapery of her unpretending couch.

We sat down—I and my beautiful hostess—and entered into earnest conversation. I examined the lady with attention. She had lost none of her former radiant beauty, and I fancied that a shade of melancholy rather enhanced her charms. Her dress was coarse and plain, but very neat, like everything else around her. Never before, in the course of my rather extensive experience, had I beheld a more interesting and fascinating woman; and never shall I forget that day, as we sat together in her little room, with the soft sunlight of a delightful May afternoon pouring in through the windows.

> "It haunts me still, though many a year has fled,
> Like some wild melody."

"My dear friend," said Mrs. Raymond, accompanying her words with a look of the deepest sympathy, "I see that you have met with a great misfortune. Pardon me, if—"

"You shall know all," said I; and then I proceeded to make her acquainted with all that had happened to me since the occurrence of the William street tragedy. Of course, I did not omit to give her the full particulars of my fatal affray with Jack Slack, as that accounted for the "great misfortune" to which she had alluded. When I had finished my narration, the lady sighed deeply and said—

"Ah, my friend, we have both been made the victims of cruel misfortune. You see me to-day penniless and destitute; I, formerly so rich, courted and admired. Have you the time and patience to listen to my melancholy story?"

I eagerly answered in the affirmative; and Mrs. Raymond spoke as follows:—

"After that terrible affair in William street—the recollection of which still curdles my blood with horror—I took up my abode in a private family at the lower end of Broadway. I soon formed the acquaintance of a gentleman of fine appearance, and agreeable address, named Livingston, who enjoyed the enviable reputation of being a person of wealth and a man of honor. I was pleased with him, and noticing my partiality, he made violent love to me. Tired of living the life of a single woman—desirous of securing a protection, and wishing to become an honorable wife instead of a mistress—I did not reject him, for he moved in the very highest circles, and seemed to be in every way unobjectionable. I will not weary you with the details of our courtship; suffice it to say that we were married. We took an elegant house in one of the up-town avenues; and, for a time, all went well. After a while, I discovered that my husband had no fortune whatever; but I loved him too well to reproach him—and besides, he had never represented himself to me as being a man of wealth; it was the circle in which he moved which had bestowed upon him that reputation. Also, I considered that my fortune was sufficient for us both. Therefore, the discovery of his poverty did not in the least diminish my regard for him. It was not long before the extensive demands which he kept constantly making upon my purse, alarmed me; I feared that he had fallen into habits of gambling; and I ventured to remonstrate with him upon his extravagance. He confessed his fault, entreated my forgiveness, and promised amendment. Of course, I forgave him; for a loving wife can forgive anything in her husband but *infidelity*. But he did *not* reform; he continued his ruinous career; and my fortune melted away like snow beneath the rays of the sun. The man possessed such an irresistible influence over me, that I never could refuse an application on his part for money. I believed that he sincerely loved me, and that was enough for me—I asked for no more. I entertained romantic notions of 'love in a cottage.'

"At length my fortune was all gone—irrevocably gone. 'No matter,' I thought —'I have still my dear husband left; nothing can ever take him away from me. I will share poverty with him, and we shall be happy together.' We gave up our splendid mansion, and sold our magnificent furniture, and rented a small but respectable house. And now my blood boils to relate how that villain Livingston served me—for he was a villain, a cool, deliberate, black- hearted one. He deserted me, carrying off with him what little money and the few jewels I still possessed, thus leaving me entirely destitute. But what added to my affliction,—nay, I should rather say my maddening rage, was a note which the base scoundrel had written and left behind him, in which he mockingly begged to be excused for his absence, and stated that he had other wives to attend to in other cities. 'I never loved you,' he wrote in that infamous letter, every word of which is branded upon my heart as with a pen of fire—'I never loved you, and my only object in marrying you was to enjoy your fortune; I have no further use for you. It may console you to know that the principal portion of the large sums of money which you gave me from time to time, was applied, not as you imagined to the payment of gambling debts, but to the support of two voluptuous mistresses of mine, whom I kept in separate establishments that were furnished with almost regal splendor. Thus did you unconsciously contribute to the existence of two rivals, who received a greater share of my attentions than you did. In conclusion, as you are now without resources, I would advise you to sell your charms to the highest bidder. There are many wealthy and amorous gentlemen in New York, who will pay you handsomely for your smiles and kisses. I shall not be jealous of their attentions to my *sixth wife*! I intend to marry six more within the next six months. Yours truly, LIVINGSTON.' Thus wrote the accursed wretch, for whom I had sacrificed everything—fortune, position in society, and friends; for who among my fashionable acquaintances, would associate with an impoverished and deserted wife? Not one. Furious at Livingston's treatment of me, I resolved to follow him, even unto the end of the earth, in order to avenge my wrongs. By careful inquiry, I learned that he had taken his departure for the western part of the state of Pennsylvania. You will hardly credit it, but it is God's truth, that being without money to pay travelling expenses, I actually set out *on foot*, and travelled through New Jersey until I reached this city. I subsisted on the road by soliciting the hospitality of the farmers, which was in most cases grudgingly and scantily bestowed, for *benevolence* is not a prominent characteristic of the New Jersey people,[F] and besides, there was certainly something rather suspicious in the idea of a well-dressed woman travelling on foot, and alone. On my arrival here in Philadelphia, I found myself worn out and exhausted by the fatiguing journey which I had performed. Having called upon some kind Quaker ladies of whose goodness I had often heard, I told them my sad history, which aroused their warmest sympathies. They placed me in this apartment, paid a month's rent in advance, purchased for me the articles of furniture which you see, and obtained for me some light employment. I worked industriously, and almost cheerfully, my object being to earn money enough to carry me to Pittsburg, in Western Pennsylvania, where, I have reason to believe, the villain has located himself.

"In my moments of leisure, I longed for some means of recreation; for I saw no company, and was very lonesome. So I wrote on to New York, and through the agency of a kind friend, had my harp sent out to me here, the rest of my poor furniture being presented to that friend. Then did the divine charm of music lighten the burden of my sorrows. One circumstance rather discouraged me: I found that with the utmost industry I could not earn more than sufficient to pay my rent and other necessary expenses, although I lived frugally, almost on bread and water, except on Sundays, when I would manage to treat myself to a cup of tea. You may smile at these trifling details, my dear friend, but I mention them to show you the hardships and privations to which poor women are often exposed. My landlady, who keeps the grocery store down stairs, is a coarse, vulgar, hard-hearted woman; and, when I was thrown out of employment in consequence of the hardness of the times, and could not pay her rent, she not only abused me dreadfully, but annoyed me by making the most infamous suggestions, proposing that I should embrace a life of prostitution, and offering to procure me plenty of 'patrons.' I, of course, indignantly repelled the horrible proposals—but, would you believe it? she actually introduced into my apartment an old, gray-haired and well-dressed libertine, for a purpose which you can easily imagine. The old villain, however, decamped when I displayed a small dagger, and declared that I would kill myself rather than become his victim. This conduct of mine still further incensed my landlady against me; and I expect every moment to be turned out into the street. It is true that I might raise a small sum of money by the sale of my harp, which is a very superior instrument, but as it was the gift of my first husband, I cannot endure the thought of parting with it, for there are associated with it some of the fondest recollections of my life. I am sure that if those kind Quaker ladies had known the character of this house and the neighborhood around it, they would not have placed me here. Heaven only knows what I have suffered, and still suffer. I live in constant dread that some ruffian, instigated by my landlady, who wishes to gratify both her avarice and malignity, may break in upon me some time when I am off my guard, and make me the victim of a brutal outrage. This fear keeps me awake nights, and makes my days miserable. Nor is this all; I have not tasted food since the day before yesterday."

"Good God!" I exclaimed—"is it possible? Oh, accursed be the circumstances which have made us both so misfortunate; and doubly accursed be that scoundrel Livingston, the author of all your sorrows. By heavens! I will seek him out, and terribly punish him for his base conduct towards you. Yes, my dear Mrs. Raymond—for such I shall continue to call you, notwithstanding your marriage to that monster Livingston—rest assured that your wrongs shall be avenged.—The villain shall rue the day when he made a play-thing of a woman's heart, robbed her of her fortune, and then left her to poverty and despair!"

[This language of mine may seem rather theatrical and romantic; but the reader will please to remember that I was only nineteen years of age at the time of its utterance—a period of life not remarkable for sobriety of language or discretion of conduct. Were that interview to take place *to-day*, I should probably thus express myself:—"My dear Mrs. Raymond, I advise you to forget the d——d rascal and put on the tea-kettle, while I rush out and negotiate for some *grub*!"]

Mrs. Raymond gratefully pressed my hand, and said—

"I thank you for thus espousing my cause;—but, my dear friend, *mine* must be the task of punishing the villain. No other hand but *mine* shall strike the blow that will send his black, polluted soul into eternity!"

These fierce words, which were pronounced with the strongest emphasis, caused me to look at my fair hostess with some degree of astonishment; and no wonder—for the quiet, elegant lady had been suddenly transferred into the enraged and revenge-thirsting woman. She looked superbly beautiful at that moment;—her cheeks glowed, her eyes sparkled, and her bosom heaved like the waves of a stormy sea.

"Well," said I—"we will discuss that matter hereafter. Have the goodness to excuse my absence for a few minutes. I have a little errand to perform."

She smiled, for she knew the nature of my errand. I went down stairs and walked up the street, in the greatest perplexity; for—let me whisper it into your ear, reader, I had not a sufficient amount of the current coin of the realm in my pockets to create a gingle upon a tomb-stone.

"What the devil shall I do?" said I to myself—"here I have constituted myself the champion and protector of a hungry lady, and haven't enough money to purchase a salt herring! Shall I *show up* my satin waistcoat? No, d——n it, that won't do, for I *must* keep up appearances. Can't I borrow a trifle from some of my friends? No, curse them, they are all as poverty-stricken as I am! I have it!—I'll test the benevolence of some *gospel-wrestler*, and borrow the devil's impudence for the occasion."

I walked rapidly into a more fashionable quarter of the city, looking attentively at every door-plate. At last I saw the name, "*Reverend Phineas Porkley*."[G] That was enough. Without a moment's hesitation I mounted the steps and rang the bell savagely. The door was opened by a fat old flunkey with a red nose of an alarming aspect. I rushed by him into the hall, dashed my hat recklessly upon the table, and shouted—

"Where's Brother Porkley? Show me to him instantly! Don't dare say he's out, for I know that he's at home! It's a matter of life and death! Woman dying—children starving—and the devil to pay generally. Wake Snakes, you fat porpoise, and conduct me to your master!"

The flunkey's red nose grew pale with astonishment and fear; yet he managed to stammer out—

"'Pon my life, sir—really, sir—Mr. Porkley, sir—he's at home, certainly, sir—in his library, sir—writing his next Sunday's sermons, sir—can't see any one, sir—"

"Catiff, conduct me to his presence!" I exclaimed, in a deep voice, after the manner of the dissatisfied brigand who desires to "mub" the false duke in his own ancestral halls.

Not daring to disobey, the trembling flunkey led the way up one flight of stairs and pointed to a door, which I abruptly opened. There, in his library, sat Brother Porkley, a monstrously fat man with a pale, oily face that contained about as much expression as the surface of a cheese.

But how was Brother Porkley engaged when I intruded upon him? Was he writing a sermon, or attentively perusing some good theological work? Neither. Oh, then perhaps the excellent man was at prayer. Wrong again. He was merely smoking a short pipe and sipping a glass of brandy and water, like a sensible man—for is it not better to take one's comfort than to play the part of a hypocrite? *I* think so.

"My dear Brother Porkley," cried I, rushing forward and grasping the astonished parson by the hand, which I shook with tremendous violence, "I come on a mission of Charity and Love! I come as a messenger of Benevolence! I come as a dove of Peace with the olive branch in my claw! Porkley, greatest philanthropist of the age, *come down*, for suffering humanity requires your assistance!"

"What do you mean, sir?" demanded the reverend Falstaff, as he vainly strove to extricate his hand from my affectionate grasp, "who are you and what do you want?"

"Brother," said I, in a broken voice, as I dashed an imaginary tear from the tip end of my nose, "in the next street there dwells a poor but pious family, consisting of a widow woman and her twelve small children. They live in a cellar, sir, one hundred feet below the surface of the earth, in the midst of darkness, horror and bull-frogs, which animals they are compelled to eat in a raw state, in order to exist. Yes *sir*!"

"But what is all this to me?"

"Much, sir, you are a Christian—a clergyman—and a trump. If you do not assist that distressed family, your reputation for benevolence will not be worth the first red cent. Those children are howling for food—bull-frogs being scarce—and that fond mother is dying of small-pox."

"Small-pox!"

"Yes *sir*! I have attended her during the last five nights, and fear that I am infected with the disease; but I am willing to lose my life in the holy cause of charity."

"Good God, sir! You will communicate the disease to *me*! Let go my hand, sir, and leave this house before you load the air with pestilence!"

"No, *sir*! I couldn't think of leaving until you have done something for the relief of that distressed widow and her twelve small children."

"D——n the distressed widow and—bless my soul! what am I saying? My good young man, what will satisfy you?"

"Five dollars, reverend sir."

"Here, then, here is the money. Now go, go quickly. Every moment that you remain here is pregnant with evil. Pray make haste!"

"But won't you come and pray with the distressed widow and her—"

"No! If I do may I be—blessed! *Will* you go!"

"I'm off, old Porkhead!"

With these words I bolted out of the library, stumbled over a corpulent cat that was quietly reposing on the landing, descended the stairs in two leaps, upset the fat flunkey in the hall, and gained the street in safety with my booty—a five dollar city bill. I hastened back towards the residence of Mrs. Raymond, but stopped at an eating-saloon on the way and loaded myself with provisions ready cooked. I did not forget to purchase two bottles of excellent wine. Thus provided, I entered the apartment of Mrs. Raymond, who received me with a smile of gratitude and joy which I shall never forget.

We sat down to the table with sharp appetites, and did full justice to the repast, which was really most excellent. The wine raised our spirits, and, forgetting our misfortunes, merrily did we chat about old times in New York, carefully omitting the slightest allusion to the bloody affair in William street. When we had finished one bottle, Mrs. Raymond favored me with an air upon her harp, which she played with exquisite skill. After executing a brilliant Italian waltz, she played and sang that plaintive song:

"The light of other days have faded,
And all their glory's past."

Just as the song was finished, there came a loud knocking at the door.

"It is my landlady," said Mrs. Raymond, in a low tone, "conceal yourself, and you will see how she treats me."

I stepped into the closet; but through a crevice in the door I could see all that transpired.

A fat, vulgar-looking woman entered with a consequential air, and a face inflamed by drink, gave her a peculiarly repulsive appearance. Of course she was utterly unconscious of my presence in the house. Taking up her position in the middle of the apartment, she placed her hands upon her hips, and said, in a hoarse and angry voice—

"Come up out o' that! *You're* a pretty one to be playing and singing, when you owe me for two months' rent. You have been feasting, too, I see. Where did you get the money? Why didn't you pay it to *me*? Have you any money left?"

"No I have not."

"Come up out o' that! Why the devil don't you sell that humstrum of yours, that harp, I mean, and raise the wind? It will bring a good ten dollars, I'll be sworn. And why don't you take my advice and earn money as other women do? You are handsome, the men would run after you like mad. That nice, rich old gentleman, Mr. Letcher, that I brought to see you, would have given you any amount of money if you had only treated him kindly—but you frightened him away. Come up out o' that! Now, what do you mean to do? I can't letyou stay here any longer unless you raise some money. This evening I'll fetch another nice gentleman here; and if you cut up any of your *tantrums* with *him*, I'll bundle you out into the street this very night."

"If you bring any man here to molest me," said Mrs. Raymond, spiritedly—"I will stab him to the heart, and then kill myself."

"Come out o' that," screamed the landlady, approaching Mrs. Raymond with a threatening look, "don't think to frighten me with your tragical airs. I must have my money, and so I'll take this harp and sell it, in spite ofyou!"

She seized upon the instrument and was about to carry it off, when I rushed forth from my place of concealment, exclaiming—

"Come up out o' that! Drop that instrument, you old harridan, or I'll drop *you*! Do not imagine that this lady is entirely friendless. I am here to protect her."

The astounded landlady put down the harp and began to mutter many apologies, for I was extremely well dressed, and she probably believed me to be some person of consequence who had become the protector and patron of Mrs. Raymond.

“Oh, sir—I'm sure, sir—I didn't mean, sir—if I had known, sir—I beg a thousand pardons, sir—”

“Come up out o' that!” cried I, “leave the room, instantly.”

The landlady vanished with a celerity that was rather remarkable, considering her extreme corpulence.

After a short pause, Mrs. Raymond said to me—

“You see to what abuse my circumstances subject me.”

“Would to God my circumstances were such as to render you that assistance you so much need; would that I could raise you from such unendurable misery! But to speak without equivocation, my condition is as penniless as your own.”

“Then you can, indeed, sympathize with my distress.”

“Most sincerely; but you must not go alone in quest of that villainous husband;—and money will be necessary.”

“This harp will—”

“Oh, no—you can never part with it.”

“I must.”

“Then let it be but temporarily. There is a pawnbroker's shop on the next square, there we can redeem it—if you can for a time endure to have it removed from your sight.”

“No matter,” said my heroine, undauntedly, “a wronged woman can endure anything when she is in pursuit of vengeance. The weather is delicious; we will travel leisurely, and have a very pleasant time. Should our money become exhausted, we will solicit the hospitality of the good old Pennsylvania farmers, who are renowned for their kindness to travellers, and who will not refuse a bite and a sup, or a night's shelter, to two poor wanderers. If you refuse to accompany me, I will go alone.”

“I will go with you to the end of the earth!” I exclaimed, with enthusiasm, for I could not help admiring the noble courage of that beautiful woman, whose splendid countenance now glowed with all the animation of anticipated vengeance.

She pressed my hand warmly, in acknowledgement of my devotion; and then, having put on her bonnet and shawl, she announced herself as being in readiness to set out.

"I have no valuables of any kind," said she, "and the landlady is welcome to this furniture, which will discharge my indebtedness to her. I shall return to this house no more."

I shouldered the harp, and we left the house without encountering the amiable landlady.

To reach the nearest pawnbroker's, it was necessary to pass through one of the principal streets. To my dismay a crowd of actors, reporters and others were assembled upon the steps of a hotel. The rascals spied me out before I could cross over; and so, putting on as bold a front as possible, I walked on pretending not to notice them, while a "running commentary," something like the following, was kept up until I was out of hearing:

"*Stag his knibbs*,"[H] said the "heavy man" of the Arch street theatre.

"Thompson, give us a tune!" bawled out a miserable wretch of a light comedian, or "walking gentleman."

"Jem Baggs, the *Wandering Minstrel*, by G——!" yelled a pitiful demon of a newspaper reporter.

"Who is that magnificent woman accompanying him?" inquired a dandy editor, raising his eye-glass and surveying my fair companion with an admiring gaze.

"Egad! she's a beauty!" cried all the fellows, in a chorus. Mrs. Raymond blushed and smiled. It was evident that these expressions of admiration were not displeasing to her.

"Excuse those gentlemen," said I to her, apologetically—"they are all particular friends of mine."

"I am not offended; indeed they are very complimentary," responded the lady, with a gay laugh. She had the most musical laugh in the world, and the most beautiful one to *look at*, for it displayed her fine, pearly teeth to the most charming advantage.

We reached the pawnbroker's and I went boldly in while Mrs. Raymond waited for me outside the door, for I did not wish her to be exposed to the mortification of being stared at by those who might be in the shop.

The pawnbroker was a gentleman of Jewish persuasion, and possessed a nose like the beak of an eagle. He took the instrument and examined it carefully,

"Vat is dish?" said he, "a harp? Oh, dat is no use. We have tousands such tings offered every day. Dere is no shecurity in mushical instruments. Vat do you want for it?"

"Ten dollars," I replied, in a tone of decision.

"Can't give it," said the Israelite—"it ish too moosh. Give you eight."

"No," said I, taking up the harp and preparing to depart.

"Here, den," said *my uncle*, "I will give you ten, but only shust to *oblishe* you —mind dat."

I duly thanked him for his willingness to *oblige* me. Uncle Moses gave me the ticket and money; and I left the shop and rejoined Mrs. Raymond, to whom I handed over the duplicate and the X.

"I will take the ticket," said she, smiling—"but you shall keep the money, for I appoint you my cashier."

At the suggestion of my fair friend we now sought out a cheap second-hand clothing establishment, which, fortunately, was kept by a woman, who, when matters were confidentially explained to her, readily entered into our plan. Mrs. Raymond and the woman retired into a rear apartment, while I remained in the shop.

Half or three-quarters of an hour passed away. At last the door of the inner apartment was opened and there entered the shop a young person whom I did not immediately recognize. This person seemed to be a very beautiful boy, neatly dressed in a cloth jacket and cap, and possessing a form of the most exquisite symmetry. This pretty and interesting lad approached me, and tapping me playfully upon the cheek, said—

"My dear fellow, how do you like me now? Have I not made a change for the better? How queenly I feel in this strange rig!"

It was of course Mrs. Raymond who addressed me. Her disguise was perfect; never before had I seen so complete a transformation, even upon the stage. No one would have suspected her to be otherwise than what she seemed, a singularly delicate and handsome boy, apparently about sixteen years of age.

I congratulated the lady upon the admirable appearance which she made in her newly adopted costume, but expressed my regret that she should have been compelled to part with her magnificent hair.

"There was no help for it," said she, laughing. "I confess that I experienced some regret when I felt my hair tumbling from my shoulders; but the loss was unavoidable, for those tresses would have betrayed my sex. This good woman, here, proved to be a very expert barber." Reflecting that a coarse suit of clothes would be just as good and better, for a dusty road, than a fine suit of broadcloth, I made a bargain with the proprietress of the shop to exchange my garments for coarse ones of fustian, she giving me a reasonable sum to counter-balance the great superiority of my wardrobe. This arrangement was speedily completed, and I found myself suddenly transformed into a rustic looking individual, who, in appearance, certainly deserved the title of a perfect "greenhorn."

All parties being satisfied, I and my fair companion departed. In the evening, having supped, we went to the theatre, where I revenged myself upon the "heavy man," and the "light comedian," who had in the afternoon made merry at my expense for carrying the harp, by getting up a hiss for the former gentleman, who knew not one single word of his part, and by hitting the latter individual upon the nose with an apple, for which latter feat (as the actor was a great favorite,) I was hounded out of the theatre, and narrowly escaped being carried to the watch-house. I and my fair friend then took lodgings for the night at a neighboring hotel.

## FOOTNOTES:

[F] Some people imagine that New Jersey belongs to the United States. That opinion I hold to be erroneous.

[G] In this, as in several other cases, I have used a fictitious name, inasmuch as a number of the persons alluded to in this narrative are still living.

[H] It is not generally known among "outsiders," that circus people and actors are in the habit of using among themselves a sort of flash language which enables them to converse about professional and other affairs without being understood by outside listeners. If I had room, I could relate many amusing anecdotes under this head. "*Stag his knibbs*" signifies "*Look at him.*"

# CHAPTER VI

***In which is introduced a celebrated Comedian from the Theatre Royal, Drury Lane, London.***

The next morning, bright and early, "two travellers might have been seen" crossing one of the ponderous bridges that lead over the Schuylkill from Philadelphia to the opposite shore. The one was a stout young cavalier, arrayed in fustian brown; the other was a pretty youth, attired in broadcloth blue, and brilliant was his flashing eye, and coal-black was his hair. By my troth, good masters, a fairer youth ne'er touched the light guitar within the boudoir of my lady.

"Now, by my knightly oath," quoth he in fustian brown, "my soul expands in the soft beauty of this rosy morn, my blood dances merrily through every vein, and I feel like eating a thundering good breakfast at the next hostelrie.— What sayest *thou*, fair youth?"

"Of a truth, Sir George," quoth he in broadcloth blue, in a voice of liquid melody, "I am hungered, and would gladly sit me down before a flagon of coffee, and a goodly platter of ham and eggs."

"Bravely spoken," quoth the stout young cavalier, with watering mouth; and then, relapsing into silence, the train journeyed onward.

Soon they paused before a goodly hostelrie, which bore upon its swinging signboard the device of "The Pig and the Snuffers."

"What ho, within there! House, house, I say!" hastily roared the youth in fustian brown, as he vigorously applied his cowhide boot to the door of the inn.

Forth came mine host of the Pig and Snuffers—a jovial knave and a right merry one, I ween, with mighty paunch and nose of ruby red. Now, by the rood! a funnier knight than this same Rupert Harmon, ne'er drew a foaming tankard of nut-brown ale, or blew a cloud from a short pipe in a chimney corner.

"Welcome, my masters—a right good welcome," quoth the fat host of the Pig and Snuffers.

"Bestir thyself, knave," quoth the cove in fustian brown, as he entered the inn followed by the pretty youth in broadcloth blue—"beshrew me, I am devilish hungry, and athirst likewise. Knave, a stoup of sack, and then let ham, eggs and coffee smoke upon the festive board!"

"To hear is to obey," said he of the Pig and Snuffers, as he waddled out of the room in order to give the necessary instructions for breakfast.

It came! Ha, ha! Shall I attempt to describe that breakfast? Nay—my powers are inadequate to the task.

But, dropping the style of my friend, G.P.R. James, the great English novelist, I shall continue my narrative in my own humble way.

We breakfasted, and cheerfully set out upon our journey. The weather was delightful; the odor of spring flowers perfumed the air, and the soft breeze made music amid the branches of the trees. On every side of us were the evidences of agricultural prosperity—fine, spacious farm-houses, immense barns, vast orchards, and myriads of thriving domestic animals. Sturdy old Dutch farmers, jogging leisurely along in their great wagons to and from the city, saluted us with a hearty "good morrow;" and one jolly old fellow who was returning home after having disposed of a quantity of produce, insisted upon giving us a "lift" in his wagon. So we got in, and about dark reached the farmer's home—a substantial and comfortable mansion that indicated its owner to be a man of considerable wealth.

I was surprised at the powers of endurance exhibited by my fair friend, who after a pretty hard day's journey, exhibited not the slightest symptom of fatigue. She kept up a most exuberant flow of spirits, and seemed delighted with the novelty of the journey which we had commenced. She was truly a charming companion, full of wit, sentiment and intelligence; and I look back upon those days with a sigh of regret—for such unalloyed happiness I shall never see again.

The good old farmer, with characteristic hospitality, declared that we should go not further that night; and we gladly availed ourselves of his kindness. He introduced us to his wife—a fine old lady, and a famous knitter of stockings —and also to his only daughter, a plump, rosy, girl about eighteen years old. This damsel surveyed my disguised companion with a look of the most intense admiration; and I saw at once that she had actually fallen in love with Mrs. Raymond!

"There will be some fun here," said I to myself—"I must keep dark and watch the movements. The idea of a woman falling love with one of her own sex, is rather rich!"

After a capital supper—ye gods, what German sausages!—I accepted the old farmer's invitation to inspect his barn, cattle, &c. My fair friend was taken possession of by the amorous Dutch damsel, who seemed to be particularly anxious to display the beauties of her *dairy*, which is always the pride of a farmer's daughter. I could not help laughing at the look of comical embarrassment which poor Mrs. Raymond assumed, when the buxom young lady seized her and dragged her off.

I of course praised the farmer's barn and stock with the air of a judge of such matters, and we returned to the house, where I applied myself to the task of entertaining the old lady, and in this I succeeded so well, that she presented me with a nice pair of stockings of her own knitting.

After a while, my fair friend and the farmer's daughter returned;—and I noticed that Mrs. Raymond looked exceedingly annoyed and perplexed, while the countenance of the Dutch damsel exhibited anger and disappointment. I could easily guess how matters stood; but, of course, I said nothing.

During the evening, my fair friend had an opportunity of speaking to me in private; and she said to me, with a deep blush, although she could not help smiling as she spoke—

"I have something to tell you which is really very awkward and ridiculous, yet you can't think how it vexes me. Now don't laugh at me in that provoking manner, but listen. That great, silly Dutch girl, after showing me her dairy, which is really a very pretty affair and well worth seeing, suddenly made the most furious love to me—supposing me, of course, to be what I seem, a boy. I was terribly confused and frightened, and knew not what to say, nor how to act. Throwing her fat arms around me, she declared that I was so handsome that she could not resist me, and that I must become her lover. I told her that I was too young to know anything about love; and then the creature volunteered to teach me all about it. Then I intimated that I could not think of marrying at present, as I was too poor to support a wife; but she laughed at the idea of matrimony, and said that she only wanted me to be her little lover. Finally I effected my release by promising to meet her about midnight, in the orchard by the gate. Now, is not all this very dreadful—to be persecuted by a big, unrelenting Dutch girl in this manner?"

I roared with laughter. It was rude and ungallant, I confess; but how could I help it? Mrs. Raymond made a desperate effort to become angry; but so ludicrous was the whole affair, that she could not resist the contagious influence of my mirth; and she, too, almost screamed with laughter.

When our mirth had somewhat subsided, I inquired—

"Well, are you going to keep an appointment with the Dutch Venus?"

"What an absurd question! Of course not! She may wait by the orchard gate all night, for what *I* care—the great, lubbery fool!"

"What do you say to *my* meeting her at the appointed time and place? I will act as your representative, and make every satisfactory explanation."

"You shall do no such thing. How dare you make such a proposition? I am perfectly astonished at your impudence!"

The next morning, after breakfast, we prepared to depart. I saw that the farmer's daughter regarded my fair friend with a ferocious look. The damsel had probably passed two or three hours in the night air, waiting for her "faithless swain."

Having thanked the good old farmer for his hospitality, and received his blessing in return, we departed.

It is not my intention to weary the reader with the details of each day's travel; indeed, my limited space would not admit of such particularity. I shall, however, as briefly as possible, relate such incidents of the journey as I may deem especially worthy of mention. When we reached Lancaster, we discovered that our funds had entirely given out, for we had livedexpensively at taverns on the way, instead of exercising a judicious economy. How to raise a fresh supply of money was now the question, and one most difficult to be answered. But an unexpected stroke of good fortune was in store for us. Strolling into the bar-room of the principal hotel, I saw a play-bill stuck up on the wall. This I read with avidity; and then, to my great satisfaction, I became aware of the fact that an old friend of mine, one Bill Pratt, a travelling actor and manager, had "just arrived in Lancaster with a talented company of comedians, who would that evening have the honor of appearing before the ladies and gentlemen of the above named place in a series of entertainments at once Moral, Chaste, Instructive and Classical, at the Town Hall. Admission—twelve-and-a-half cents."

So read the play-bill. I and my fair friend immediately posted to the Town Hall, and there I found Brother Pratt busily engaged in arranging his stage, putting up his scenery, &c. He was prodigiously glad to see me.[1] Among his company I recognized several old acquaintances. I introduced my travelling companion to the ladies and gentlemen of the profession; and I do not think that any of them suspected her true sex. We all dined together at the hotel; and a merry party we certainly were, "within the limits of becoming mirth." Wit sparkled, conundrums puzzled, bad puns checked, and rich jokes awoke the laughing echoes of the old dining-hall. Happy people are those travelling actors—happy because they are careless, and, in the enjoyment of to-day, think not of the morrow. Are they not true philosophers?

> "Oh, what's the use of sighing,
> Since time is on the wing—

To-morrow we'll be dying,
So merrily, merrily sing—
Tra, la, la!"

After dining in company with Brother Pratt I seated myself upon the piazza; and, while we smoked our cheroots, we recalled the past, dwelt upon the present, and anticipated the future.

After a considerable amount of desultory conversation, the Brother suddenly asked me—

"Who is that handsome little fellow with whom you are travelling?"

"Oh, he ran away from home in order to see something of the world, as well as to avoid being apprenticed to a laborious trade," was my reply, for I did not consider it at all necessary to let my friend into the secret.

"He's a lad of spirit, and I like him," rejoined the Brother. "If he went upon the stage, what a splendid court page he'd make! But where are you going? Tell me all about it."

I told the Brother all that was necessary for him to know.

"And so," said he, reflectively, "you are entirely out of funds. That's bad. We must raise you some cash, in some way or other. I will immediately cause bills to be printed, announcing that 'the manager has the pleasure of informing his numerous patrons that he has, at enormous expense, succeeded in effecting a brief engagement with Mr. George Thompson, the celebrated comedian from the Theatre Royal, Drury Lane, London, who will make his first appearance in his celebrated character of Robert Macaire, in the great drama of that name, as performed by him upwards of two hundred nights before crowded and fashionable audiences including the royalty, nobility and gentry of England, who greeted him with the most terrific and enthusiastic yells of applause, and Her Majesty the Queen was so delighted with the masterly and brilliant representation, that she presented Mr. Thompson with a magnificent diamond ring valued at five thousand pounds sterling, which ring will be exhibited to the audience at the conclusion of the performance.' How will *that* do, my boy? We'll raise the price of admission to twenty-five cents on account of the extra attraction. I'll play Jaques Strop, the house will be crammed, and you will go on your way rejoicing, with a full pocket."

"I say, old fellow," I gravely remarked—"are you not laying it on a *little too thick*?"

"Not at all," coolly replied the brother as he carefully knocked the ashes off the end of his cigar, "not at all. Humbug is the order of the day. I'll get a flashy ring to represent the one presented to you by the queen. You know enough about stage business to play the part of Robert Macaire very respectably and you also know that I am not very slow in Jaques Strop. You'll make a hit, depend on it. I'll get you the book, and you can look over the part. What you don't learn you can gag.[J] I'll announce you for to-morrow night. Leave all to me; I'll arrange everything. Let's go in and drink!"

I was soon master of the part; and, at the end of the next day's rehearsal, I was found to be "dead letter perfect." The manager and the members of his company congratulated me on the success which I was sure to meet with. Meanwhile, the town had been flooded with bills, which made the same extravagant announcement that Brother Pratt had suggested to me. Public expectation and curiosity were worked up to the highest pitch; and a crowd of excited people assembled in front of the principal hotel, in anticipation of the sudden arrival of the "distinguished comedian" in a splendid coach drawn by four superb white horses, and attended by a retinue of servants in magnificent livery.

Evening came, and the large hall was crowded almost to suffocation, although the price of tickets had been doubled. I was full of confidence, having fortified myself by imbibing several glasses of brandy and water. Just before going on the stage Brother Pratt was, to use a common expression, "pretty well over the bay." Well, to make a long story as short as possible, I went on at the proper time, followed by Jaques Strop. My appearance was greeted with a perfect whirlwind of applause, which lasted four or five minutes. Taking off my dilapidated beaver, I gracefully bowed my thanks and then began the part which commences thus:

> "Come along, comrade, put your best leg foremost. What are you afraid of? We are out of danger now, and shall soon reach the frontier."

I may say without egotism, that I got through the part remarkably well, and I certainly kept the audience in a continual roar of laughter. Mrs. Raymond occupied a front seat;—and her encouraging smile sustained me throughout the play. When the piece was over, I was loudly called for.

"Now, my boy," said Brother Pratt to me, "go in front of the curtain and make a rip-staving speech—I know you can do it. Say that at the urgent solicitation of the manager, you have consented to appear to-morrow night as Jem Baggs, in the Wandering Minstrel."

"Very good," said I, "but these people will now want to see the ring which Queen Victoria presented to me. How shall I manage that?"

"Easy enough," replied the Brother, as he drew from his pocket and handed me a big brass ring ornamented with a piece of common glass about the size of a hen's egg.

Out I stepped in front of the curtain. A bouquet as large as a cabbage struck me in the face, and fell at my feet. The giver of this delicate compliment was an ancient female very youthfully dressed. I picked up the bouquet, and pressed it to my heart. This was affecting, it melted the audience to tears. Silence having been obtained, I made a bombastic speech, which Brother Pratt afterwards declared to be the best he had ever heard delivered in front of the "green baize." I spoke of being a stranger in a strange land, of the warm welcome which I received, of eternal gratitude, of bearing with me beyond the ocean the remembrance of their kindness, admitted that I was closely allied to the British aristocracy, but declared that my sentiments were purely republican and in favor of the "Star-Spangled Banner."

Here there was a tempest of applause and when it had subsided, the orchestra, consisting of a fiddle and a bass-drum, struck up the favorite national air which my words had suggested. Then I exhibited the diamond ring which had been presented to me by the Queen of England; and, as the spectators viewed the royal gift, the most profound silence prevailed among them. When I had sufficiently gratified them by displaying the lump of brass and glass, I remarked that I would appear on the next evening as Jem Baggs in the Wandering Minstrel. This announcement was received with shouts of approbation; and bowing almost to the foot-lights, I withdrew.

The next night, the audience was equally large and enthusiastic, and my "farewell speech" was so deeply affecting, that there was not a dry eye in the house.

Brother Pratt urged me to become a regular member of his company; but, although he offered me a good salary, and glowingly depicted the pleasant life of a strolling player, I declined, not having any ambition in that way. Besides, it was my duty to get on to Pittsburg with Mrs. Raymond, without any unnecessary delay.

Having received nearly fifty dollars as my share of the proceeds, I took my leave of Brother Pratt and his company; and, accompanied, of course, by my fair friend, resumed my journey.

I wish I had sufficient time and space to describe all the adventures through which we passed, prior to our arrival in Pittsburg. But such details would occupy too much room, and I must make the most of the few pages that are left for me to occupy.

We crossed the Alleghanies, and, taking the canal at Johnstown, soon reached Pittsburg. Here we made some essential improvements in our garments, and put up at a respectable hotel, Mrs. Raymond still sustaining her masculine character.

By diligent inquiry, we learned that the villain, Livingston, was in the city; and my fair friend prepared to avenge the base wrongs which he had inflicted upon her.

## FOOTNOTES:

[I] All who have the good fortune to know Bill Pratt *alias* "The Original Beader," will acknowledge that a wittier, funnier or better man never breathed.

[J] This word, in theatrical parlance, signifies "to employ language which the author of the play never wrote."

---

# CHAPTER VII

***A deed of blood and horror.***

We had no difficulty in ascertaining the place of Livingston's abode; for he was well known in the city. He resided in a handsome house situated on one of the principal streets; and we discovered that the lawless rascal was actually engaged in the practice of the law!

"My dear friend," said Mrs. Raymond to me one day, as we were strolling along the banks of the river, "I will not suffer you to involve yourself in any trouble on my account. You must have nothing to do with this Livingston. You must remain entirely in the back-ground. To me belongs the task of punishing him. I tell you frankly that I shall kill the man. He is not fit to live, and he must not be permitted to continue his career of villainy. Whatever may be my fate, do not, I entreat you, by unhappy on my account. When I have shed the heart's blood of Livingston, I shall be willing to die upon the scaffold. To the very last moment of my life, I shall cherish for you a sentiment of the most affectionate gratitude; you sacrificed all your own plans in order to accompany me here, and, throughout the entire long journey, you have treated me with a degree of kindness and attention, which I can never forget while life remains. But a truce to melancholy; let us change the subject."

"With all my heart," said I; and leaving the river side, we walked up into the centre of the city.

We passed an elegant dwelling-house on the door of which was a silver plate bearing the name "Livingston." This was the residence of the villain who ruined Mrs. Raymond.

A carriage drove up before the door, and from it leaped a tall, fine-looking man, dressed in the height of fashion. He assisted a beautiful and elegantly attired lady to alight from the vehicle, and conducted her into the house.

"That man is Livingston, and that woman must be *one of his wives*," said Mrs. Raymond, with a bitter smile, as she placed her hand in her bosom, where, I knew, she carried a dirk-knife.

"My friend," resumed she, after a pause, "leave me; I may as well perform my bloody task now, as at any other time. I will invent some pretext for requesting an interview with Livingston, and then, without uttering a single word, I will stab him to the heart. Farewell, forget me, and be happy!"

"Stay," said I—"you must not leave me thus. Let me persuade you to abandon, at least for the present, your terrible design with reference to Livingston. You are agitated, excited; wait until you are cool, and capable of sober reflections."

Mrs. Raymond regarded me with a look of anger, as she said, passionately—

"And was it for the purpose of giving me such advice as *this*, that you accompanied me from Philadelphia to this city? You knew, all the while, the object of my journey, and yet now, in the eleventh hour, when an excellent opportunity presents itself for the accomplishment of that object, you seek to dissuade me from my purpose. Have I entirely mistaken your character? Are you really as weak-minded, and as devoid of courage and spirit, as your language would seem to indicate? When that young ruffian mutilated you in Philadelphia, didn't you consider that you acted perfectly right? Well, this Livingston has destroyed the happiness of my life, and transformed me from a lady of wealth into a penniless beggar. Say does he not deserve to *die*?"

"Why—yes," was my reluctant reply—"but then it seems too terrible to go about the horrible business deliberately, and in cold blood."

"He coolly and deliberately planned and effected the ruin of my peace, happiness and fortune," rejoined Mrs. Raymond, in a tone of fixed determination—"and it is therefore but just that he should be coolly and deliberately slain. Once more, farewell; by everything sacred, I swear that you shall not turn me from my purpose. My regard for you is great—but, if you seek to detain me by force, your heart shall be made acquainted with the point of my knife!"

"I have no idea of using force," said I, reproachfully—"but, if I *had*, no such threat as the one which you have just now made, would deter me. Go, my friend, go—do as you will; but I will go with you, for I swear that I will not leave you."

This announcement deeply affected Mrs. Raymond, who embraced me and begged my pardon for the language which she had used.

"Forgive me, my best, my only friend," said she—"the loyalty and devotion which you have always manifested towards me should have prompted different expressions.—If you are *determined* to accompany me, and see me through this business, *follow me*."

I obeyed, hoping to be able to prevent the perpetration of the terrible deed which she meditated.

She rang the bell at the door, which was opened by a servant.

"I wish to see your master, instantly, on particular business," said the disguised woman.

"What name, sir?" demanded the servant.

"It matters not. Say to Mr. Livingston that two gentlemen wish to see him on business of the greatest importance."

The servant disappeared, but soon returned, saying that she would conduct us to her master.

We followed her into a handsomely furnished library, where Mr. Livingston was seated, looking over some letters. He glanced at us carelessly, and said—

"Well, young gentlemen, what can I do for you to-day? Do you wish to consult me on any matter of law? I am entirely at your service."

It was evident that the villain did not recognize the woman whom he had so basely wronged.

Mrs. Raymond uttered not one single word, but, thrusting her hand into her bosom, she slowly approached the author of her ruin, who still continued to peruse his letters in entire unconsciousness of the terrible danger that hung over him.

I watched Mrs. Raymond with the closest attention, fully determined to spring forward at the critical moment and prevent the desperate woman from accomplishing her deadly purpose.

It was a deeply interesting and thrilling scene, and one which I shall never forget. There sat the intended victim, whose soul was hovering on the awful precincts of an endless eternity; there stood the avenger of her own wrongs, her right hand nervously grasping the hilt of the weapon in her bosom, her face deadly pale, and her eyes flashing with wild excitement. And there I stood, trembling with agitation, and ready to spring forward at the proper time to prevent the consummation of a bloody tragedy.

Mr. Livingston suddenly looked up from his letters, and started when he beheld the pale and wrathful countenance of Mrs. Raymond, whose eyes were fixed upon him with an expression of the most deadly hatred.

"Your face seems strongly familiar to me; have we not met before?" asked Livingston.

"Yes," calmly replied Mrs. Raymond—"we *have* met before."

"That voice!" cried the doomed villain—"surely I know it. Who are you, and what want you with me?"

"I am the victim of your treacherous villainy, and I want revenge!" screamed

Mrs. Raymond, as, with the quickness of lightning, and before I could prevent her, she drew her weapon and plunged it into the heart of Livingston, who fell from his chair to the floor and died instantly.

"Now I am satisfied," said the woman, as she coolly wiped the blood from the blade of her knife.

Language cannot depict the horror which the contemplation of this bloody deed caused within me. True, I had myself slain a human being—but then it was done in self-defence, and amid all the heat and excitement of a personal contest. *This* deed, on the contrary, had been committed, coolly and deliberately; and, although Mrs. Raymond's wrongs were undoubtedly very great, I really could not find it in my heart to justify her in what she had done.

How bitterly I reproached myself for not having adopted some effectual means of hindering the performance of that appalling deed, even at the risk of incurring Mrs. Raymond's severe and eternal displeasure! I felt myself to be in some measure an accessory to the crime; and I feared the law would, at all events, consider me as such.

"What is done cannot be helped now," said I to Mrs. Raymond, who stood calmly surveying the body of her victim—"come let us leave the house and seek safety in flight. We may possibly escape the consequence of this bloody act."

"No," said the woman—"*I* shall not stir an inch. I have relieved the world of a monster, and now I am ready to receive my reward, even if it be the scaffold. But go, my friend—go, and secure your own safety."

"No, I will not leave you, even if I have to share your fate," was my reply. That was a very foolish determination, I admit; for how could my remaining with her, do her any good? I was merely placing myself in a position of the utmost peril. But I thought it wrong to desert Mrs. Raymond in that dark and trying hour; and therefore, as she refused to escape, I resolved to remain with her.

Some one softly opened the door, and a female voice said—

"My dear, are you particularly engaged? May I come in?"

Hearing no reply, the fair speaker entered with a smile on her rosy lips. This lady was the newly-made wife of Livingston. She had been, of course, in happy ignorance of his true character, and of the fact that he was already the husband of several wives.

On seeing us, she evinced surprise, for she knew not of her husband having visitors. Suddenly, her eyes fell upon Livingston's bleeding corpse, which lay upon the floor. On seeing this horrid spectacle, she gave utterance to a piercing scream, and fell down insensible.

That shrill, agonizing scream penetrated every part of the house, and brought all the inmates to the library, to see what had happened. Horror took possession of the group, as they gazed upon the awful scene. For a few minutes, there reigned the most profound silence. This was at last broken by one of the male servants, who demanded—

"Who has done this?"

"I did it," replied Mrs. Raymond, calmly, "I alone am guilty. Here is the weapon with which I did the deed. This young man here is entirely innocent; he tried to prevent the act, but I was too quick for him. Let me be conveyed at once to prison."

Officers being sent for, soon arrived and took us both into custody, notwithstanding the passionate protestations of Mrs. Raymond that I had no hand whatever in the affair.

"That must be shown to the satisfaction of higher authorities than we are," said one of the officers. "At all events, it is our duty to secure this young man as a witness. If he is innocent, he will doubtless be able to prove it."

Half an hour afterwards, I was an inmate of the Pittsburg jail, in an apartment adjoining that occupied by Mrs. Raymond, whose real sex still remained undiscovered.

---

# CHAPTER VIII

### *An Escape, and a Triumph.*

After a few weeks' incarceration, Mrs. Raymond, in accordance with my advice, made known the secret of her sex to the chief officer of the prison, to whom she also communicated the great wrongs which she had suffered at the hand of Livingston. The officer, who was a good and humane man, was deeply affected by this narrative. He immediately placed Mrs. Raymond in a more comfortable room and caused her to be provided with an abundance of female garments, which she now resumed. Her story, of course, was given in all the newspapers; and it excited the deepest sympathy in her behalf. One editor boldly asserted that no jury could be found to convict the fair prisoner under the circumstances. As regarded my case, the propriety of my immediate discharge from custody was strongly urged, an opinion in which I fully concurred.

I shall dwell upon these matters as briefly as possible. I was first brought to trial, and the jury acquitted me without leaving their seats; Mrs. Raymond was merely convicted of manslaughter in the fourth degree, so great was the sympathy that existed in her behalf, and the judge sentenced her to be imprisoned during the term of two years. Although I considered her particularly fortunate in receiving a punishment so comparatively light, I resolved to effect her liberation in some way or other.

I may as well here remark that the last wife and victim of Livingston never survived the blow. She soon died of a broken heart.

My first step was to repair to Harrisburg, the capitol city of the State, in order to solicit Mrs. Raymond's pardon from Governor Porter, who was renowned, and by some parties strongly condemned, for his constant willingness to bestow executive clemency upon prisoners convicted of the most serious offences.[K] I easily obtained an interview with his Excellency, whom I found to be a very clever sort of personage. Having made known my errand, and related all the particulars of Mrs. Raymond's case, I urged her claims to mercy with all the eloquence of which I was master.

The Governor listened to me with attention; and, when I had concluded, he said—

"My inclination strongly prompts me to pardon this most unfortunate lady; but I have recently pardoned so many convicted prisoners, that the press and the people generally are down on me, and I really dare not grant any more pardons at present. I will, however, commute the lady's sentence from two years to one."

With this partial concession I was obliged to be contented. The necessary documents were made out, and with them I posted back to Pittsburg. When I entered the cell of my fair friend and told her what I had effected in her behalf, she burst into tears of gratitude and joy. One long year taken off her sentence, was certainly something worth considering.

"Courage, my friend!" said I, "even if you are obliged to serve out the remnant of your sentence, which I trust will not be the case, a year will soon pass away. I shall not leave Pittsburg until you are free. You will see me often; and I will take care that you are abundantly provided with everything that can contribute to your comfort. Keep up a good heart; you have at least one friend who will never desert you."

Three months passed away, during which time I gained an excellent subsistence by writing for various newspapers and magazines. Three times every week I had an interview with Mrs. Raymond, whom I caused to be supplied with every comfort and luxury as allowed by the rules of the prison. She had just nine months to serve, when one day I was unexpectedly enabled to effect her liberation in the following manner.

I had called upon her, as usual. After an interview of about half an hour's duration, I bade her adieu and left her apartment. To gain the street, it was necessary to pass through the office of the prison. In that office were generally seated three or four turnkeys, one of whom always went and locked Mrs. Raymond's door after my leaving her.

Upon entering the office on the occasion to which I now refer, I found but one turnkey there, and he was *fast asleep*. I instantly resolved to take advantage of the lucky circumstance which good fortune had thrown in my way.

Hastening back to Mrs. Raymond's cell, I briefly told her the state of affairs and bade her follow me. She obeyed, as might be supposed, without much reluctance. We passed through the office and out into the street; but, before departing, I transferred the key from the inside to the outside of the door and locked the sleeping turnkey in, so that there could be no possibility of his immediately pursuing us, when he should awaken and discover the flight of his prisoner.

I was tolerably well furnished with cash, and my fair friend, at my suggestion, purchased an elegant bonnet and shawl—for, it will be remembered, she had resumed the garments appropriate to the female sex. As for myself, I was exceedingly well dressed, and no alteration in my costume was necessary, in order to present a respectable appearance.

I entertained no serious apprehensions of any great effort being made to capture the fugitive, she having had but nine months to serve, and being therefore a person of but little importance when viewed as a prisoner. Moreover, I hoped that the kind-hearted chief officer of the prison would charitably refrain from making any extraordinary exertions in the matter. But these considerations did not prevent me from exercising a reasonable degree of caution.

We left Pittsburg that evening, for Philadelphia, where we arrived in due season. I immediately sought and procured employment as a writer, at a liberal salary. A few days after our arrival in Philadelphia, Mrs. Raymond said to me—

"My dear friend, I am not going to remain a burden to you. Listen to the plan which I have to propose. I think of going upon the stage."

"What, and becoming an actress?"

"Yes. I flatter myself that my voice and figure are both passable; and I really think that I possess some talent for the theatrical profession. A respectable actress always receives a good salary. If the plan meets with your approbation, I shall place myself under the tuition of some competent teacher; and my *debut* shall be made as soon as advisable."

I did not attempt to dissuade Mrs. Raymond from carrying out this plan, which I thought, in fact, to be a very excellent idea. Once successfully brought out upon the stage, she would have a profession which would be to her an unfailing means of support.

According to the best of my judgment, she possessed every mental and physical qualification necessary to constitute a good actress. Beautiful and sprightly, talented and accomplished—possessing, too, the most exquisite taste and skill as a vocalist and musician, I saw no reason why she should not succeed upon the stage as well, and far better, than many women a thousand times less talented. Therefore, encouraged by my cordial approbation of her plan, and acting in accordance with my recommendation, the fair aspirant to dramatic honors placed herself under the instructions of a popular and well-known actor, who was fully capable of the task which he had undertaken.

A few months passed away, and my fair friend announced herself as being nearly in readiness to make her first appearance. I was delighted with the rapid and satisfactory progress which she had made. The recitations with which she occasionally favored me, were delivered in the highest style of the elocutionary art, and convinced me that she was destined to meet with the most unbounded success.

She proposed making her *debut* as *Beatrice*, in Shakespeare's glorious comedy, "Much Ado About Nothing,"—a character well calculated to display her arch vivacity and charming sprightliness. I saw her rehearse the part, and was satisfied that she *must* achieve a brilliant triumph,—an opinion that was fully concurred in by her gratified instructor, and also by the manager and several of the leading actors and actresses of the theatre.

The eventful evening came at last, and the house was crowded in every part. Seating myself in a private box in company with the actor who had instructed Mrs. Raymond, I awaited her appearance with the utmost confidence. The curtain arose, and the play commenced. When *Beatrice* came on, a perfect storm of applause saluted her. Her appearance, in her elegant and costly stage costume, was really superb. Perfectly self-possessed, and undaunted by the sea of faces spread out before her, she went on with her part, and was frequently interrupted by deafening shouts of approval. The *Benedict* of the evening being a very fine actor, and the *Dogberry* being as funny a dog as ever created a broad grin or a hearty laugh—the entire comedy passed off in the most admirable manner; and, at its conclusion, my fair friend being loudly called for, she was led out in front of the curtain by *Benedict*. A shower of bouquets now saluted her; and, having gracefully acknowledged the kindness of the audience, she retired.

This decided success caused the manager to engage Mrs. Raymond at a liberal salary. She subsequently appeared with equal success in a round of the best characters; and the press, and every tongue, became eloquent in her praise. She was now in a fair way to acquire a fortune as great as the one which she had lost through the villainy of Livingston.

Thinking her worthy of a higher position than that of a mere stock actress, I advised her, after a year's sojourn in Philadelphia, to travel as a *star*. To this she eagerly assented, and accordingly I accompanied her to New York, where she was immediately engaged by the late Thomas S. Hamblin, of the Bowery Theatre.[L] Her success at this popular establishment was unprecedented in the annals of dramatic triumphs. Night after night was she greeted by crowded, enthusiastic and enraptured audiences. In short, she became one of the most celebrated actresses of the day.

## FOOTNOTES:

[K] It is related of Governor Porter as an illustration of his pardoning propensities, that once, after his term of office had expired, a gentleman accidentally ran against him in the street. “I beg your pardon,” said the gentleman. “I cannot grant it,” said Mr. Porter, “for I am no longer Governor.”

[L] I have not, for reasons that will be easily understood, given the name which Mrs. Raymond assumed, after her adoption of the dramatic profession.

# CHAPTER IX

***An accident—a suicide—and a change of residence.***

A dreadful accident abruptly terminated Mrs. Raymond's brilliant professional career. One night, while she was dressing in her private room at the theatre, a camphene lamp exploded and her face was shockingly burned. Her beauty was destroyed forever, and her career upon the stage was ended. Thus was the public deprived of a most delightful source of entertainment, and thus was a popular actress thrown out of the profession just as she had reached the pinnacle of fame, and just as she was in a fair way to acquire a handsome fortune.

It would be impossible for me to describe the grief, consternation and horror of the unfortunate lady, on account of this melancholy accident. In vain did I attempt to console her, she refused to be comforted. She abandoned herself to despair; and I caused her to be closely and constantly watched, fearing that she might attempt to commit suicide.

The play-going public soon found a new idol, and poor Mrs. Raymond was forgotten. Her face was terribly disfigured, and it was very fortunate that her sight was not destroyed. When she became well enough, she endeavored to gain a situation as a teacher of music; but she was unceremoniously rejected by every person to whom she applied, on account of the repulsiveness of her countenance. This of course, still further increased the dark despair that overshadowed her soul.

"My friend," said she to me one day, "I shall not long survive this terrible misfortune. My heart is breaking, and death will ere long put an end to my sufferings."

"Come, come," said I, "where is your philosophy? Have you not passed through trials as great as this? While there is life, there is hope; and you will be happy yet."

I uttered these commonplace expressions because I knew not what else to say. Mrs. Raymond replied, with a mournful smile—

"Ah! with all your knowledge of the world, you know not how a woman feels when she has been suddenly deprived of her beauty. The miser who loses his wealth—the fond mother from whom death snatches away her darling child; these bereaved ones do not feel their losses more acutely than does a once lovely woman feel the loss of her charms. Do not talk to me of philosophy, for such language is mockery."

I visited my unfortunate and no longer fair friend very often, but all my attempts to cheer her up signally failed. She persisted in declaring that she was not long for this world; and I began to believe so myself, for she failed rapidly. I saw that she was provided with every comfort; but alas! happiness was beyond her reach forever.

One evening I set out to pay her a visit. On my arrival at the house in which she had taken apartments, the landlady informed me that she had not seen Mrs. Raymond during the whole of that day.

"It is very singular," remarked the woman, "I knocked five or six times at the door of her chamber, but she gave me no answer, although I know she has not gone out."

These words caused a dreadful misgiving to seize me. Fearing that something terrible had happened, I rushed up stairs, and knocked loudly upon the door of Mrs. Raymond's chamber. No answer being returned, I burst open the door, and my worst fears were realized, for there, upon the floor lay the lifeless form of that most unfortunate woman. She had committed suicide by taking arsenic.

This dreadful event afflicted me more deeply than any other occurrence of my life. I had become attached to Mrs. Raymond on account of a certain congeniality of disposition between us. We had travelled far together, and shared great dangers. That was another link to bind us together. Besides I admired her for her talent, and more particularly for her heroic resolution. She was, altogether, a most extraordinary woman, and, under the circumstances, it was no wonder that her tragical end should have caused within me a feeling of the most profound sorrow.

Having followed her remains to their last resting-place, I did something that I was very accustomed to do—I sat down to indulge in a little serious reflection, the result of which was that I determined to go to Boston, for New York had become wearisome to me. Besides, I knew that Boston was the grand storehouse of American literature—the "Athens of America," and I doubted not my ability to achieve both fame and money there.

To Boston I accordingly went. On the first day of my arrival, I crossed over to Charlestown for the purpose of viewing the Bunker Hill Monument. Having satisfied my curiosity, I strolled into a printing office, fell into conversation with the proprietor, and the result was that I found myself engaged at a moderate salary to edit and take the entire charge of a long-established weekly newspaper of limited circulation, entitled the "Bunker Hill Aurora and Boston Mirror." This journal soon began to increase both in reputation and circulation, for I filled it with good original tales and with sprightly editorials. Yet no credit was awarded to me, for my name never appeared in connection with my productions, and people imagined that W——, the proprietor, was the author of the improvements which had taken place.

"Egad!" the subscribers to the *Aurora* would say—"old W—— has waked up at last. His paper is now full of tip-top reading, whereas it was formerly not worth house-room!"

How many instances of this kind have I seen—of writers toiling with their pens and brains for the benefit and credit of ungrateful wretches without intellect, or soul, or honor, or common humanity! Charlestown is probably the meanest and most contemptible place in the whole universe—totally unfit to be the dwelling-place of any man who calls himself *white*. The inhabitants all belong to the *Paul Pry* family. A stranger goes among them, and forthwith inquisitive whispers concerning him begin to float about like feathers in the air. "Who is he? What is he? Where did he come from? What's his business? *Has he got any money?* (Great emphasis is laid on this question.) Is he married, or single? What are his habits? Is he a temperance man? Does he smoke—does he drink—does he chew? Does he go to meeting on Sundays? What religious denomination does he belong to? What are his politics? Does he use profane language? What time does he go to bed—and what time does he get up? Wonder what he had for dinner to-day?" &c., &c., &c.

During my residence in Charlestown, where I lived three years, I became acquainted with the celebrated editor and wit, Corporal Streeter, who was my next-door neighbor. I dwelt, by the way, in an old-fashioned house situated on Wood street. Two ancient pear trees sadly waved their branches in front of the house, and they are still there, unless some despoiling hand has cut them down—which Heaven forbid! If ever I re-visit that place, I shall gaze with reverence at the old house—for in it I passed some of the happiest days of my life. The antique edifice I christened "The Hermitage." The squalling cats of that neighborhood afforded me a fine opportunity for pistol practice.

At the end of three years, I had a slight "misunderstanding" with Mr. W——, the proprietor of the Aurora, one of the most stupendously mean men it was ever my misfortune to encounter. He was worthy of being the owner of the only newspaper in Charlestown, alias, "Hogtown." Having civilly requested Mr. W—— to go to the devil at his earliest convenience, I left him and his rookery in disgust, and shifted my quarters over to Boston.

Here I engaged largely in literary pursuits, and began to write a series of novels. These were well received by the public, as every Bostonian will recollect.

In my next chapter, I shall tell the reader how a gentleman got into difficulties.

# CHAPTER X

### *Six weeks in Leverett Street Jail.*

A popular actor who was a personal friend of mine[M] took a farewell benefit at the National Theatre. At his invitation, and just before the close of the evening's performances, I attempted to enter the stage door for his purpose of seeing him in his dressing-room, as he intended to sup with me and several friends. A half-drunken Irishman attached to the stage department in some menial capacity, stopped me and insolently ordered me out. I treated the Greek, of course, with the contempt which he merited, whereupon he called another overgrown bog-trotter to his assistance, and the twain forthwith attacked me with great fury. Finding myself in danger of receiving rather rough treatment, I drew a small pocket pistol and aimed at their shins, being determined that one of them, at least, should hobble around upon crutches for a short time. The cap on the pistol, however, refused to explode, and the two vagabonds immediately caused me to be arrested, charging me with "assault and battery with the intent to kill!" I was forthwith accommodated with a private apartment in Leverett Street jail, where I remained six weeks, during which time I enjoyed myself tolerably well, being amply provided with good dinners, not prison fare, but from the outside, candles, newspapers, books, writing materials, &c. During my imprisonment, I wrote "The Gay Deceiver," and "Venus in Boston." My next door neighbor was no less a personage than Dr. John W. Webster, who was afterwards executed for the murder of Dr. Parkman. Webster was a great glutton, and thought of nothing but his stomach, even up to the very hour of his death. On account of his "position in society," (!) every officer of the prison became his waiter; and a certain ruffianly turnkey, who was in the habit of abusing poor prisoners in the most outrageous manner, would fawn to the Doctor like a hungry dog to a benevolent butcher.

Webster was very polite to me, frequently sending me books and newspapers —favors which I as often reciprocated. He once sent me a jar of preserves, a box of sardines and a bottle of wine. The latter gift I highly appreciated, wines and liquors of every kind being prohibited luxuries. That night I became very happy and jovial; but I did not leave the house.

Dr. Webster was confident of being acquitted; but the result proved how terribly he was mistaken. Probably, in the annals of criminal jurisprudence, there never was seen a more striking instance of equal and exact justice, than was afforded by the trial, conviction and execution of John W. Webster.

Money, influential friends, able counsel, prayers, petitions, the *prestige* of a scientific reputation failed to save him from that fate which he merited as well as if he had been the most obscure individual in existence.

After six weeks imprisonment, I was brought to trial before Chief Justice Wells. I was defended by a very tolerable lawyer, to whom I paid twenty-five dollars in consideration of his conversing five minutes with a jury of my peers, the said jury consisting of twelve hungry individuals who wanted to go out to dinner. When my legal adviser had made a few well-meaning remarks, the jury retired to talk the matter over among themselves; and, after about fifteen minutes absence, they returned and expressed their opinion that I was "not guilty." This opinion induced me to believe that they were very sensible fellows indeed. Not for a moment did I think of demanding a new trial; that would have been impertinent, as doubting the sagacity of the jury. My two Irish prosecutors left the court-room in a rage; and two more chop-fallen disappointed and mortified Greeks were never seen. The Judge took his departure, the spectators dispersed, and I crossed the street and dined sumptuously at Parker's, with a large party of friends.

Very many of my Boston readers will remember a long series of articles which I wrote and published about that time, in the columns of one of the newspapers, entitled "Mysteries of Leverett Street Jail." In those sketches I gave the arrangements of the Jail, and its officers, "particular fits;" and the manner in which the fellows writhed under the inflictions, was a caution to petty tyrants generally. The startling revelations which I made created great excitement throughout the whole community; and I have good reason to believe that those exposures were the means of producing a far better state of affairs in the interior of the "stone jug."

I have thus, very briefly, given the extent of my experience with reference to the old Leverett Street Jail. Unlawful ladies and gentlemen are now accommodated in an elegant establishment in Cambridge street, for the old Jail has been levelled to the ground to make room for "modern improvements."—I visited it just before the commencement of its destruction, and gazed at my old apartment "more in sorrow than in anger." There were my name and a few verses, which I had written upon the wall. There was the rude table, upon which I had penned two novels, which, from their tone, seem rather to have emanated from a gilded *boudoir*. There, too, in the grated window, was a little flower-pot in which I had cultivated a solitary plant. That poor plant had withered and died long ago, for the prisoners who succeeded me probably had no taste for such "trash." I took and carefully preserved the dead remains of my floral favorite—"for," said I to myself—"they will serve to remind me of a dark spot in my existence."

And now, with the reader's permission, I will turn to matters of a more cheerful character.

## FOOTNOTES:

[M] I allude to Mr. W.G. Jones, now deceased.

# CHAPTER XI

### *"The Uncles and Nephews."*

Ring up the curtain! Room there for the Boston Players. Let them approach our presence, not as they appear upon the stage, in rouge, and spangles, and wigs, and calves and cotton pad; but as they look in broad daylight, or in the bar-room when the play is over, arrayed in garments of a modern date, wearing their own personal faces, swearing their own private oaths, and drinking real malt out of honest pewter, instead of imbibing dusty atmosphere from pasteboard goblets. Room, I say!

There is an intimate connection between the press and the stage, that is a congeniality of character, habit, taste, feeling and disposition, between the writer and the actor. The press and the stage are, in a measure, dependent on each other. The newspaper looks to the theatre for light, racy and readable items, with which to adorn its columns, like festoons of flowers gracefully hung around columns of marble. The theatre looks to the newspaper for impartial criticisms and laudatory notices. Show me a convivial party of actors, and I will swear there are at least two or three professional writers among them. I know many actors who are practical printers, fellows who can wield a composing-stick as deftly as a fighting sword. Long life and prosperity to the whole of them, say I; and bless them for a careless, happy, pleasure-loving, bill-hating and beer-imbibing race of men. Amen.

There is one point of resemblance between the hero of the sock and buskin and the Knight of the quill. The former dresses up his person and adopts the language of another, in order to represent a certain character; the latter clothes his ideas in an appropriate garb of words, and puts sentiments in the mouths of his characters which are not always his own. But I was speaking of the Boston Players.

Admitting the foregoing argument to be correct, it is not to be wondered at that I became extensively acquainted among the members of the theatrical profession. My name was upon the free list of every theatre in the city; and every night I visited one or more of the houses—not to see the play, but to chat in the saloons with the actors and literary people who in those places most did congregate. After the play was over, we all used to assemble in an ale-house near the principal theatre; and daylight would often surprise us in the midst of our "devotions." A curious mixed-up set we were to be sure! I will try to recollect the most prominent members of our club. First of all there was the argumentative and positive Jim Prior, who might properly be regarded as President of the club. Then came H.W. Fenno, Esq., the gentlemanly Treasurer of the National. He, however, seldom tarried after having once "put the party through." The eccentric "Old Spear" was generally present, seated in an obscure corner smoking a solitary cigar. Comical S.D. Johnson and his hopeful son George were usually on hand to enliven the scene; and so was Jim Ring, alias J. Henry, the best negro performer, next to Daddy Rice, in the United States. Chunkey Monroe, who did the villains at the National; and, towering above him might be seen his cousin, Lengthy Monroe, who enacted the hard old codgers at the same establishment. That fine fellow, Ned Sandford, must not be forgotten; neither must Sam Lake, the clever little dancer. Rube Meer was invariably to be found in company with a pot of malt; and he was usually assisted by P. Jones, a personage who never allowed himself to be funny until he had consumed four pints. Charley Saunders, the comedian and dramatist, the author of "Rosina Meadows" and many other popular plays—kept the "table in a roar," by his wit and also by his excruciatingly bad puns. Bird, of "Pea-nut Palace" notoriety, held forth in nasal accents to Bill Colwell, the husband of the pretty and accomplished Anna Cruise. Big Sam Johnson, a heavy actor, a gallant Hibernian and a splendid fellow, discussed old Jamaica with his friend and boon companion, Sam Palmer, alias "Chucks." The mysterious Frank Whitman captures his brother-actor at the Museum, Jack Adams, and imprisoning him in a corner from which there was no escape, imparts to him the most tremendous secrets. Ned Wilkings—one of the best reporters in the city—tells the last "funny thing" to John Young; while Joe Bradley, proprietor of the Mail, touches glasses with Jim McKinney. Meanwhile, the two waiters, Handiboe and Abbott, circulate around with the greatest activity, fetching on the liquors and removing the dirty glasses, from which they slyly contrive to drain a few drops now and then, for their bodily refreshment. As an instance of the "base uses" to which genius may "come at last," I will state that Handiboe, whom we now find in such a menial position, was once quite a literary character; while poor Abbott, to whom I now throw a few small coins in charity, was a setter of type. The rest of the party is made up of Pete Cunningham, Sam Glenn, Bill Dimond, Jim Brand, Bill Donaldson, Dan Townsend, Jack Weaver, Cal Smith, and a host of others whom it would puzzle the very devil himself to remember.

Such was the "Uncle and Nephew Club," of which I had the honor to be a prominent member. Almost every man belonging to it was a wit, a punster or a humorist of some kind; and I will venture to say, that had some industrious individual taken the pains to preserve and publish one-half the good things that were said at our meetings, a large volume might be formed that would be no contemptible specimen of genius. Whenever a member had the audacity to perpetrate some shocking bad pun, and such enormities were frequent, the offender was sentenced to undergo some ludicrous punishment; and the utmost good-humor and hilarity always prevailed.

I will now relate a rather amusing adventure in which I participated with others of the "Uncles and Nephews."

One night we were assembled, as usual, at our head-quarters. The Fourth of July was to "come off" the next day, and we determined to have some fun. Accordingly, a couple of stout messengers were despatched to the theatre, armed with the necessary authority and keys, and they soon returned laden with dresses from the wardrobe. These garments the party proceeded to assume; and we were quickly transformed into as picturesque-looking a crowd as any that ever figured at a masquerade ball. As for myself, I made a very tolerable representation of Falstaff; while Richard, Othello, Macbeth, Hamlet, Shylock, and other gentlemen of Shakespeare's creation, gave variety to the procession. Then there was a clown in full circus costume, accompanied by Harlequin in his glittering shape-dress. We sadly longed for a sprightly Columbine; but then we consoled ourselves with Pantaloon, admirably rendered by P. Jones.

Our "music" consisted of a bass-drum, which was tortured by the clown; a fish-horn beautifully played upon by Sam Palmer; a dinner-bell whose din was extracted by Jack Adams. Having formed the procession on the side- walk, the music struck up, and we marched.

Our first halting-place was at the saloon of Peter Brigham, at the head of Hanover street. Here we filed in, and great excitement did our extraordinary appearance create. A mob soon collected before the door, attracted by our grotesque costumes as well as by the infernal noise of our "musical" instruments, upon which we continued to perform with undiminished vigor. Peter Brigham was in agonies, and rushed about the saloon like an insane fly in a tar barrel. The frightened waiters abandoned their posts and fled. The mob outside cheered vociferously; and Harlequin began to belabor poor Pantaloon with his gilded lath to the immense amusement of the spectators.

Peter Brigham at length mounted a chair, and said—

"Gentlemen, will you hear me? (Hoarse growl from the bass-drum.) I cannot suffer this noise and racket to go on in my house. (Blast of defiance from the fish-horn.) You know I have always tried to keep a decent and respectable place. (Peal of sarcastic laughter from the dinner bell.) I have a proposition to make.—(Hear! hear!) If you will promise to leave the house quietly, I will treat you all to as much champagne as you can drink." (Yell of acceptance from the bass-drum, fish-horn and dinner-bell! Great excitement generally.)

The wine was produced, and the facility with which it was disposed of, caused Mr. Brigham to stare. He endured its consumption, however, with the most philosophical fortitude, until we began to drink toasts, make speeches, and exhibit other indications of a design on our part to "tarry yet awhile." Peter then reminded us of our promise; and, as gentlemen of honor, we fulfilled the same by immediately falling into procession and marching out of the saloon. Away we went down Hanover street, followed by the admiring and hooting crowd. We entered the establishment of Theodore Johnson, and were hospitably received by the prince of good fellows, who, assisted by Chris Anderson, "did the honors" with the utmost liberality. Sam Palmer and P. Jones, here favored the company with a broad-sword combat; after which I, as Falstaff, gave a few recitations—the performances concluded with Abbott as *Jocks*, the Brazilian ape. Our next visit was to the Pemberton House, then under the control of Uriah W. Carr, a very small man, both physically and morally. Uriah received us very churlishly, and peremptorily refused to"come down" with the hospitality of the season. He was particularly down on me for having once written and published some verses concerning him. The following is all that I can recollect of that interesting production:—

"Tis comical, indeed it is
To see him mix a punch—
He puts two drops of liquor in,
And then he eyes the *lunch*;
truts about most pompously,
Then stands before the fire,
Just like a little bantam-cock,
This comical Uriah!"

Inasmuch as Uriah refused to bring on the "bush" for either love or money, we determined to help ourselves. Therefore, every man appointed himself a bar-keeper *pro tem*. Wines, liquors and cigars were disposed of with marvelous celerity, and poor little Uriah danced about and tore his hair in the agony of his spirits. Meanwhile, a large number of actors and others, boarding at the Pemberton, joined us, being ushered in by Charles Dibden Pitt, a performer of great elegance and power, then playing a brilliant star engagement—at the Museum. This gentleman is decidedly "one of the boys," and goes in for a "good time." At his suggestion, a committee was appointed to descend to the kitchen and bring up provisions. Ned Abbot and Bill Ball performed this duty in the most admirable and satisfactory manner. They departed for the lower regions, and soon returned laden both with substantials and delicacies. Then, such a feast!—or, rather, such a banquet! Champagne flowed like water, for we had discovered a closet filled with baskets of the foaming beverage. The whole company was of course soon in a state of glorious elevation. The song and jest went round unceasingly, and peals of jovial laughter trooped away like merry elves upon the midnight air. We were in excellent humor to adopt the prayer of the following who said—

"Oh, let us linger late to-night,
Nor part while wit and song are bright;
And, Joshua, make the sun stand still,
That we of joy may have our fill!"

There was one gentleman who refused to participate in the festivities of the occasion. This was little Uriah, the landlord, who gazed upon the progress of the banquet with a troubled brow; yet he did not dare to openly remonstrate, through fear of offending Mr. Pitt, and other valuable boarders.

Unfortunately for the harmony of the festival, a party of drunken students from Cambridge dropped in, and I instantly saw that a row was inevitable. After unceremoniously helping themselves to drink, the students gazed at our strange-looking company superciliously, and one of them remarked with a sneer—

"What fools are these, dressed up in this absurd manner? Oh, they must be monkies, the property of some enterprising organ-grinder. Let them dance before me, for my soul is heavy, and I would be gay!"

Here little Billy Eaton, the writer, who was one of our party, fired up and obligingly offered to fight and whip the man with the heavy soul, for and in consideration of the trifling sum of one cent. This handsome offer was accepted; but, before the gentlemen could strip for the combat, a general collision took place between all the hostile parties. Chairs were brandished, canes were flourished and decanters were hurled, to the great destruction of mirrors and other fragile property. The bar was overturned, and the din of battle was awful to hear. Notwithstanding the uproar and confusion that prevailed, I could not help noticing poor Uriah, who, in the dimly-lighted hall, was quietly dancing an insane polka, accompanying his movements by low howls of despair. The little man had temporarily lost his few wits, that was plain. The combat raged with undiminished fury. Our clown attacked a student with his bass-drum, one end of which burst in, imprisoning the representative of the seat of learning, who found it impossible to extricate himself from his musical predicament. Sam Palmer, with his fish-horn, did tremendous execution; while Jack Adams was equally effective with his dinner-bell which, at every blow, sounded forth a note of warning. The heroic
P. Jones performed prodigies of valor, and covered himself with glory. This wonderful young man, having planted himself behind a rampart of chairs,

placed himself in the position of a pugilistic frog, and boldly defied his enemies to "come on and be punched." At the commencement of the fight, Abbott coiled himself up under the table, and was seen no more; while Handiboe fled for safety to the cole-hole. The battle was at its height, and the bird of victory seemed about to perch upon the banner of the "Uncles and Nephews," when some reckless, hardened individual turned off the gas, thus producing total darkness. This made matters ten times worse than ever, for it was impossible to distinguish friends from foes. Suddenly, in rushed a posse of watchmen, headed by the renowned Marshal Tukey, and bearing torches. Many of the combatants were arrested, and but few contrived to make their escape. I had the honor of figuring among the unlucky ones; and, with my companions passed the night in durance vile. In the morning, when day light feebly penetrated our gloomy dungeon, what a strange-looking spectacle presented itself! Stretched upon the floor in every imaginable picturesque attitude, were about a score of men, the majority of them arrayed in the soiled and torn theatrical dresses. These unhappy individuals afforded a most melancholy sight, as many of them had black eyes, bruised noses and battered visages.

"D——d pretty fools we've made of ourselves," said Macbeth, one of whose optics had been highly discolored.

"Yes," groaned Othello, whose black eyes were only partially concealed by the yellow color which he had smeared over his face—"and here we are in the jug, where we shall be compelled to remain all day, and lose all the fun of the Fourth of July."

"That isn't the worst of it," sighed Hamlet, whose royal frontispiece had received severe damage—"I am on the bills to play twice this afternoon and once this evening, and my being absent will cause me to be *forfeited*, if not discharged. D——n those college students! What the devil became of them? They all got clear, I suppose."

"No," said I—"they are in a separate apartment. Of course the officers would not put them in with us, for that would be encouraging a renewal of the fight."

"My head aches horribly," remarked Richard, Duke of Gloster—"I would give my kingdom for a drink!"

"And I," observed Shylock—"would like a pound of flesh, providing it were beefsteak, for I am almost famished."

"Hah! what a hog!" growled Cardinal Richelieu, one side of whose face had been "cove in" most dreadfully—"to think of *eating* at such a time as this!"

"Hark," said Claude Melnott, whose handsome countenance had been knocked completely out of shape, and who looked as if he had just returned from the wars rather the worse for wear; "hark! Don't you hear the sound of artillery, and of music? The ceremonies and festivities of the glorious day have commenced. Would to Heaven that I were with Pauline, in our palace on the lake of Como!"

"Dry up, you fool!" angrily exclaimed the aged and venerable King Lear, whose nasal organ exhibited signs of its having sustained a violent contusion —"I haven't closed an eye during the whole night, and now you keep me awake with your infernal jabbering. Shut up, I say!"

"Oh, shut up be blowed!" said P. Jones—"how can a man shut up when he thinks of the good *budge* (rum) he loses by being shut up here? Rube Meer, isn't this too bad?"

"Worse than the time when I sent on a fishing excursion with Jim Morse," groaned poor Rube, as he fumbled in his pocket for a match with which to light his pipe, "has anybody got a rope with which a fellow could contrive to hang himself?"

"I say, Jack Adams," said Sam Palmer, who was dressed as Don Caesar de Bezas, "what will Harry Smith and old Kimball say, when we don't make our appearance to-day, the busiest day in the whole year?"

"I care not," replied Jack, as he fondly pressed the portrait of his Katy to his lips, "so long as this blessed consolation is left me, the world may do its worst! Frown on, ye fiends of misfortune! I defy ye all, so long as my Katy Darling remains but true!"

"That's the one!" shouted the bold Dick Brown, as "usher" at the National Theatre, "let us have the song of Katy Darling, and all join in the chorus."

This was done; and from the depths of that gloomy dungeon rolled forth the words, in tones of thunder—

"Did they tell thee I was false, Katy Darling?"

Suddenly, to our great joy, the ponderous iron door of the dungeon was unlocked and thrown open, and an officer announced that he had orders to release us all, provided that we would engage to satisfy the landlord of the Pemberton House for the damage he had sustained. This we of course agreed to do, it being understood that the college students should be compelled to pay one-half the amount, which was certainly no more than right, as they had perpetrated half the damage, and had commenced the row in the first place. The landlord having received sufficient security that his damages would be made whole, we were all set at liberty, to our most intense delight, for we had anticipated being imprisoned during the whole of that glorious day.

We left the house of bondage, and, as we passed through the already crowded streets, our fantastic dresses and strange appearance generally, collected a mob at our heels, which, in broad daylight, was certainly rather annoying. However, we soon reached the theatre, and resumed our own proper habiliments.

It was announced upon the bills of the theatre that a certain actor would that evening deliver an original Fourth of July poem. That poem I had engaged to write, yet not a single line had I committed to paper. The actor was in a terrible quandary, and swore that his failure to recite the poem, as announced, would render him unpopular with the public and ruin him forever. Telling him to keep cool and call again in two hours, I sat down to my writing-desk and dashed off a poem of considerable length. My pen flew with the rapidity of lightning, words and ideas crowded upon me in overwhelming numbers, and in three-quarters of an hour my work was done! I sent for the actor who was astonished at the brief space of time in which I had performed the task. Having heard me read the poem, he declared himself to be delighted with it; and, with all due humility and modesty, I must say that the production did possess considerable merit. I had avoided the usual stereotyped allusions to the "star spangled banner," to the "Ameri-eagle," to the "blood of our forefathers," &c.;—and had dwelt principally upon the sublime moral spectacle afforded by an oppressed people arising in their might to throw off the yoke of bondage and assert their independence as a nation. The actor soon committed the poem to memory; and, having rehearsed it over to me and found himself perfect, he departed. That night he recited it from the stage to a dense audience; and, during its delivery and at its conclusion, I had the satisfaction of listening to the most delicious music that an author's ears can ever know, the clapping of hands, and deafening peals of applause.

---

# CONCLUSION

## *My Parting Bow.*

Several years have passed since the date of the events last narrated. Those years have been crowded with adventures full as extraordinary as those already detailed; but alas! neither time nor space will at present, admit of my giving them to the public. Perhaps, at some future time, I may make up for this deficiency, if my life is spared.

The reader may rest assured of one thing:—that *not one single word of fiction or exaggeration has been introduced into these pages*. Why should I wander in the realms of romance, when there are more startling facts at my command than I can possibly make use of? Is not truth stranger than fiction? Every day's experience proves such to be the case.

I cannot close up these pages without availing myself of the opportunity to return my thanks in this public manner, to several gentlemen from whom I have received courtesies and acts of kindness. First and foremost, there is Jerry Etheridge, a man of great political influence and historical learning. To this distinguished gentleman I am indebted for an act of generosity that rescued me from a serious embarrassment. I am not the only recipient of his bounty, for I know many others who have applied to him in times of need, and who have left him, encouraged by his cheering words and relieved by his liberality. He is one of those true philanthropists who never publish their good deeds to others. I consider that when one man befriends another and then tells of it, all obligation ceases to exist between the parties, and no gratitude is due the one who confers the benefit, which he bestows, perhaps just on purpose to acquire a reputation for whole-souled benevolence, and not out of any particular good-will to the other. I am also under obligation to Mr. W.R. GOODALL, the promising young American actor, who will one day, I predict, occupy a most elevated position in the profession which he has adopted, and for which he is peculiarly qualified. Who that ever heard his famous imitations, as Jeremiah Clip, will hesitate to admit that he is a young man of the most extraordinary talent? NED SANDFORD and JIM LANERGAN, both of whom are now while I write this, playing at the Broadway Theatre, I return my most sincere thanks for favors received; and I trust that they will pardon me for making this public allusion to them. Finally, to every person who has, through disinterested motive, treated me with kindness and consideration, I would say—friends, your goodness shall never be forgotten while life remains.

I have many bitter enemies, and they will, I presume, continue to snarl at my heels like mongrel curs. Their miserable attempts to injure me will only rebound back upon themselves. I am above the reach of their malignity, and shall pursue my own independent course regardless of their spleen.

Nearly one year has now elapsed since I left Boston—a place that I cannot but regard with some degree of affectionate remembrance; for, with all its faults, I like it still.

It is possible that I may hereafter continue to write tales for the public amusement. Should I conclude to continue in my business as a writer, I shall always, as heretofore, labor to produce that which is interesting, exciting and founded on truth, and entirely unobjectionable in a moral point of view. Unlike many so-called writers who throw off a quantity of trash and care not how it fills up space, I am always willing to bestow time and toil upon my work, for the sake of my own credit, for the purpose of securing the rapid and extensive sale of the book—and in order to give the public perfect satisfaction.

Reader, fare thee well! We may never meet again; but I thank thee for accompanying me from the beginning to

**THE END**

www.ingramcontent.com/pod-product-compliance
Lightning Source LLC
Chambersburg PA
CBHW060801310726
48980CB00002B/186
* 9 7 8 3 7 3 2 6 2 9 6 5 7 *